Hot Winter
Nights

CODI GARY is an obsessive bookworm, who likes to write sexy contemporary romances with humour, grand gestures, and blushworthy moments. When she's not writing, she can be found reading her favourite authors, squealing over her must-watch shows, and playing with her children. She lives in Idaho with her family.

BOOK**SHOTS**

STORIES AT THE SPEED OF LIFE

What you are holding in your hands right now is no ordinary book, it's a BookShot.

BookShots are page-turning stories by James Patterson and other writers that can be read in one sitting.

Each and every one is fast-paced, 100% story-driven; a shot of pure entertainment guaranteed to satisfy.

Available as new, compact paperbacks, ebooks and audio, everywhere books are sold.

BookShots – the ultimate form of storytelling. From the ultimate storyteller.

Hot Winter Nights

CODI GARY

BOOK**SHOTS**

1 3 5 7 9 10 8 6 4 2

BookShots
20 Vauxhall Bridge Road
London SW1V 2SA

BookShots is part of the Penguin Random House group of companies
whose addresses can be found at global.penguinrandomhouse.com.

Penguin
Random House
UK

First published by BookShots in 2016

www.penguin.co.uk

A CIP catalogue record for this book is available from the British Library.

ISBN 9781786530738

Printed and bound in Great Britain by Clays Ltd, St Ives Plc

FOREWORD

When I first had the idea for BookShots, I knew that I wanted to include romantic stories. The whole point of BookShots is to give people lightning-fast reads that completely capture them for just a couple of hours in their day—so publishing romance felt right.

I have a lot of respect for romance authors. I took a stab at the genre when I wrote *Suzanne's Diary for Nicholas*. While I was happy with the results, I learned that the process of writing those stories requires hard work and dedication.

That's why I wanted to pair up with the best romance authors for BookShots. I work with writers who know how to draw emotions out of their characters, all while catapulting their plots forward.

You're about to fall into a plot that doesn't stop. All of us enjoy a good love story between a fated couple. In *Hot Winter Nights,* Codi Gary raises the stakes by tempting her heroine, Allie Fairchild, with two strapping men. Who will she choose? I guess you'll have to race through these pages to find out....

James Patterson

Hot Winter Nights

Chapter 1

ALLIE FAIRCHILD STARED out her windshield at the ramshackle cabin.

Please tell me I have the wrong address.

Scrambling for the MapQuest printout amid the fast-food bags and other evidence that she had blown her diet once again, she read the directions over and over. Finally, sure that she hadn't misinterpreted them, she looked up at what had been described to her as "charming and rustic." She was pretty sure it had been the setting for her favorite horror movie, *The Cabin in the Woods.*

In fact, she half expected to see flesh-eating zombies pop out from behind the thick pine trees surrounding it. When her landlord, Dex Belmont, had warned her that they were a few miles outside of Bear Mountain, Montana, he had definitely been bending the truth a bit. According to her car's odometer, she was a good ten miles from the town limits on a curvy road that had made her stomach queasy....

And in the middle of the freaking forests of Narnia.

Leaning her head on the steering wheel of her Jetta, she groaned in defeat. After thirty-two years, she had thought that she was making a solid choice for once. She'd planned to come to small-town Montana to turn a poorly run trauma center into one of the best in the country, and therefore erase all of the potholes in life she'd been unable to avoid thus far.

"Hoooooooooooowwwwwllll!"

Allie jumped a foot in the air, shrieking. Outside her window was a huge hound with its mouth practically pressed to the glass, vibrating her door with its deep bellow.

"Bluebell!" a deep voice said loudly, out of sight. The car-shaking sound stopped and the dog sat, its hot breath fogging her window. Allie's hand gripped the front of her blouse, sure her heart was going to pound its way right out of her chest.

Suddenly, her passenger door opened and a man peeked in.

"Sorry if she scared you. She likes to be the welcoming committee."

Allie blinked, taking in a head of tousled, sun-streaked brown hair and green eyes set in a tanned, gorgeous face. The man's smile was wide and boyish, completely dispelling her previous surprise and terror. The muscles of his shoulders stretched the lightweight T-shirt he was wearing, and the brief flash of a tattoo beneath the sleeve tempted her to reach out to get a better look.

"Do you always spring out at people like a serial killer?"

His golden eyebrows rose, but he didn't lose that smile. "Not usually, but we've been waiting for you."

Clearing her throat, she said unconvincingly, "Yeah, that isn't helping your whole stalker vibe."

He held his hand out to her, hovering over the center console. "I'm Dex Belmont. Allie, right?"

This guy was her landlord? Taking his hand hesitantly, she tried to ignore the pleasant warmth of his palm against hers. He had lured her out to his property with a bunch of misleading photos, after all. None of the shots of this cabin had shown an iffy-looking roof or a porch that was missing a sturdy railing.

"Yeah, I'm Allie, and I have a bone to pick with you—"

"Hang on, before you start picking, why don't I come around and get your door?"

"I can get my own door, thank you very"—he slammed her passenger side door before she finished and was coming around the front—"much."

She reached for the handle at the same time he did, and when he pulled it open, she practically fell out on her face, putting her nose-to-nose with his dog. Big, droopy brown eyes stared at her from inches away, and then a large, wet tongue smothered her nose with slobber.

Mustering whatever dignity she had left, she started to climb to her feet, shaking off his hands as he attempted to help. Swiping at her nose with her arm, she glared up at him. Wow, he was tall. She liked tall.

She shook away her thoughts and said, "This is not at all what you promised me. You told me that the cabin was 'cozy'—"

"Look, I may have tweaked the truth a bit, but you're also here two weeks earlier than I was expecting." He crossed his arms in front of his chest, and Allie tried to ignore the way the muscles flexed as he scowled down at her as if she were the one who had bait-and-switched him. "So, before you start throwing a walleyed fit, how about you take a look inside and I'll tell you about all the improvements I'll be making?"

If Allie was smart, she'd get her butt back in her car and hightail it out of there, but this had been the only place for rent, according to the realtor she'd spoken to over the phone. She could buy a place, but she hadn't been ready for that kind of commitment. She wanted to take a few months and get used to Bear Mountain before she actually bought something.

And the few motels she'd passed hadn't looked better than this.

"Fine. Lead the way, McDuff."

That smile was back in place, doing crazy things to her insides, although her outsides were freezing. She rubbed the arms of her lightweight sweater. "How are you only wearing a T-shirt? I wasn't expecting it to be so cold already."

"We start getting snow around mid-October, but so far we've been storm-free." He glanced back at her over his shoulder and she finally understood exactly what the word *smolder* meant. "And as to my attire, my temperature runs hot. Wanna feel?"

"Get real."

Dex chuckled as he climbed up onto the porch. "You never told me why you decided to move from New York to Bear Mountain. I can't imagine it was for the culture."

Allie hesitated in answering when the first porch step squeaked loudly under her foot. "Are you sure I'm not going to fall through here?"

"Front porches squeak, I promise. The first thing I did was start on the porch, so I've already reinforced and replaced a lot of it." He stood at the top of the steps and held his hand down to her. "I won't let anything happen to you."

Despite the temptation, she ignored his hand and walked past him, her shoulder brushing the front of his shirt. She snuck a glance at the hard outline of his chest, swallowing.

"You were just going to tell me why you left home?"

"I needed a fresh start and figured rural Montana was as good a place as any for a change."

"What exactly will you be doing here?" he asked, holding the front door open for her.

"I'm running Bear Mountain Memorial Hospital."

He seemed skeptical. "You're awfully young to take on such a big job."

"If I'd wanted to work in a state-of-the-art hospital, I could have, but I wanted to go where I could really help people." She didn't want to throw charity events or expensive dinners just to "Save the Otters," like her parents did. "As for my qualifications, I have a double major in business and nursing, with a master's degree in hospital administration. I may look young, but I have experience. I know what I'm doing, Mr. Belmont."

When she turned back toward the door, his arm shot out, blocking her way. He leaned down until their faces were only a few inches apart, and her palms started sweating as her heart thumped.

"Why don't you just call me Dex?"

Chapter 2

DEX BELMONT WAITED for Allie to hightail it back into her car and take off, but she just stood there, her pretty brown eyes never flickering away. He could tell he affected her, but he didn't know whether it was because he pissed her off or because she was attracted to him, and he was more than tempted to find out which.

That wouldn't be a smart move on his part, especially since she would be living next door. She'd get attached, and once she found out he wasn't the kind of guy for a long-term relationship, drama would ensue.

And he was over drama.

"Are you going to show me the cabin or kiss me, Dex?"

Her question sent a shock wave of awareness through him, and for a second, he thought it was a proposition. Until…

"Fair warning: if you attempt the latter, I know six easy moves that will leave you broken and bleeding on the floor."

Picturing this short, curvy woman bringing him low made

him burst out laughing. He dropped his arm and let her pass. "I like the brass on you, Allie."

She frowned as she surveyed the kitchen, and he could tell she wasn't happy with its current state. Hell, he couldn't blame her one bit. The place did look like shit, but he was supposed to have had more time. She'd called him a week ago and said she wouldn't be arriving until the first week of November. Then two days ago, she'd called again from Nebraska to let him know she'd be there two weeks ahead of schedule.

"I know it looks bad, but really, there are no leaks and I'll have it looking brand new in just a few weeks. You know, the few weeks I would have had if you'd given me more notice?"

"Fine, you have a point," she said. "I shouldn't have changed the game plan on you like that, but with all the work I have to get done at the hospital and with the weather report saying that it's supposed to get bad soon, there didn't seem to be any time to waste. Plus, I have to get to know the doctors and nurses, and judging by *some* people's reaction to my age and gender, I can't imagine all of them will be too welcoming."

Dex nearly choked as he tried to hold in his laughter. Including his best friend, Hunter, there were four trauma surgeons at the hospital who were all seasoned military vets. He could just imagine how they were going to react to this curvy blonde with just the slightest New York accent walking in there and pointing out everything they were doing wrong.

Actually, he'd pay money to see that…or at least charge admission.

"Yeah, that's true. If you want to whip that place into shape, you will definitely need a firm hand and a good night's rest, which won't be a problem. She might not look like much, but this cabin's sturdy and safe. I'm putting up the new porch railing this weekend, but like I said, I reinforced the deck, so there's no problem there."

Dex saw that she was staring up at the hole in the ceiling and could feel warmth steal up his neck. Okay, so he felt a little guilty for misleading her, but when Heather Dolan at the real estate office had asked him if his cabin was ready to be rented, he'd jumped at the chance to get a little extra scratch during the winter months. Not that he was struggling, but he liked to have a nest egg, something he'd learned from his parents. It was about the only thing he'd inherited from his mathematician father and psychology professor mother. As a child, he'd had to beg his friends' dads to take him along on their camping trips, while his parents had preferred museums and working on their latest publications.

Of course they had loved him, but they'd never really understood his love of the outdoors. Or his decision to become a search-and-rescue specialist after eight years in the army. He'd stopped trying to explain it years ago, and just let it be. He was happy, financially stable, and doing what he loved. His parents came to visit a couple of times a year and spent most their time doting on his quiet, bookish younger brother. It worked.

That being said, if his mother ever found out he'd been less than forthcoming with his current tenant, he'd be in for a damn long lecture on ethics and honesty.

Maybe that was why he was so defensive with the irritated woman standing before him.

"I'll be fixing that, too," he said.

Allie crossed her arms under her breasts and he tried like hell not to look down as she berated him. "I can't believe you rented this place to me in this condition. Even if I had told you I wouldn't be here in three months, the amount of work this place needs…"

She turned away from him as she trailed off, her gaze scanning the room again, taking in all the things that were wrong with the place. Dex knew for a fact that the repairs weren't as extensive as she assumed. He'd had a contractor out months ago to give him an estimate, but Dex had sent him on his merry way. Dex could do everything he'd listed for a quarter of the guy's "conservative estimate."

"Wow, so you're a construction worker, too?" he asked.

She turned those big brown eyes on him. "No, but I don't need to be to tell you this place needs a lot of work."

"Not as much as you think, sweetheart. A little patch here and a bit of paint there, and it will be grand." His fake Irish accent didn't even crack the skeptical look on her face. He'd never met a woman immune to it before.

"I'm sure you think so, but until you get the repairs done, I'm withholding rent."

Outrage blazed through Dex and he took a step toward her. "Now, just one damn minute—"

"No, *Mr. Belmont*"—the way she exaggerated his name, he knew it was meant to rankle him—"you already admitted that the cabin isn't ready for me. I may have had a change of plans, but when I called two days ago, you could have told me the truth and I would have made other arrangements. As it stands, I am not going to pay you to live in a place that probably has a leaky roof, because you weren't honest. Now, you can tell me to get the hell off your property, and I will be happy to find a hotel while I search for another place to live. Or you can get started on the repairs right away, and as soon as they're complete, I'll reinstate our original agreement."

Then she actually smiled at him like she'd invited him over for tea.

"So what do you say? Do I stay or do I go?"

Chapter 3

HUNTER GRACIN PULLED on his blue scrubs, tying the knot quickly. He was running late this morning, and couldn't afford to piss off the new director of Bear Mountain Memorial Hospital. God only knew he'd tested Bill Featherton, the previous director, more times than he could count when he'd come here after finishing his residency in his home state of Texas. It didn't help that old Bill had been a bullheaded dick too tightfisted to update a single machine in the place during his reign.

Hunter hoped that the new director was actually here to work and make a change, and wasn't using Bear Mountain as a placeholder until he retired.

No one knew anything about this guy except that he was from New York. Hunter couldn't figure out why some big-city dude would move to the-middle-of-nowhere Montana. Maybe he was originally from the area and wanted to come home.

Grabbing his stethoscope and lab coat, Hunter ran down

the hallway to the room where the staff was supposed to gather for the formal introduction. He could speculate all he wanted, but if he didn't get his ass front and center before the bigwig started talking, he might not have a job at all.

He pushed in next to Jay Cromwell, who glanced his way briefly before facing forward once more. Jay was a large man of few words, except when he got a couple of glasses of whisky in him. Then he wouldn't shut up. Both of them had served in the armed forces, and it had been an instant bond with them and the other two doctors on staff.

"Rough night?" Jay asked quietly.

"Nah, just forgot to charge my phone, so my alarm didn't go off."

"You're lucky she's not here yet."

Hunter paused as he shrugged into his lab coat, surprised. "Our new director is a woman?"

"Apparently."

Hunter grinned, imagining the kind of woman that would come in and whip their asses into shape. Sadly, in his mind she looked a bit like his fourth-grade teacher, Mrs. Harvel, who had sounded as if she smoked six packs a day and looked like she could bench-press a Buick. Hunter had to admit it would be nice to get a younger woman in town, though. The women they had were either married, too young, or about twenty years older than his thirty-four years. As fun as cougars were, he was ready to settle down. He wanted someone he could have kids and grow old with.

"Holy shit," Jay hissed.

Hunter tried to follow his line of vision, but there were too many people in the way. And then, suddenly, a young blonde in a purple silky blouse and black slacks stepped up onto the stairs, smiling out at the crowd.

"Good morning, everyone. My name is Allison Fairchild and I will be taking over as director of Bear Mountain Memorial Hospital.

"What does that mean for you? Well, for starters, I want to assure you that there will be no layoffs; your jobs are safe. However, we will be working to update the equipment and computer system. My goal is to help Bear Mountain become one of the best trauma centers in the country, and to do that, I'm going to need all of your cooperation to make sure the changes I will be implementing are seamless. I will be conducting interviews with all of you, as a way to introduce myself to you and address any of your concerns. Again, I appreciate you all being here today and look forward to working with you. Thank you."

As she stepped down out of sight, Jay whistled. "Damn, she's a lot more fun to look at than grizzled Bill, am I right?"

Hunter couldn't have agreed more, and as the crowd dispersed, a buzz of excitement continued sparking him as he went about his work, waiting for Allison Fairchild to call him into her office.

Just after lunch, his pager went off and he made his way to the administration floor. When he reached the room that used to be Bill's office, he knocked on the door.

"Come in."

Hunter stepped inside and got a good look at Allie Fairchild. From thirty feet away, she had been pretty, but now, she was gut-punchingly gorgeous.

She stood up and gave him a smile, and Hunter caught the signs of tension around her eyes.

"Dr. Gracin, please take a seat."

"After you, ma'am. I might be a doctor, but I'm a gentleman first."

Her smile brightened. "Thank you. I have to admit, you're the only person who doesn't seem to think my presence is a sign of the apocalypse."

Hunter laughed, waiting until she was fully seated before he did the same.

"I'm sorry if they're giving you a rough time. I think most of us were expecting someone a little more—"

"Male?" Her tone wasn't bitter, simply matter-of-fact.

"Actually, I was going to say aged."

She laughed, opening what he assumed was his file. "I assure you, Dr. Gracin, that although I may not be as 'aged' as you may have hoped, I am perfectly capable and qualified to take Bear Mountain to the next level."

"I don't doubt you one bit, Ms. Fairchild. And if anyone else gives you any trouble, I say to hell with them. We could use some new blood." He gave her his best grin before adding, "Especially someone who brightens up the room."

She looked up from the file, her head cocked to the side. "Are you flirting with me, Dr. Gracin?"

"No, ma'am, that would be unprofessional. But, seeing as how you're new and in need of someone to show you around, I thought I'd offer myself up. I'd be happy to take you to dinner one of these nights, show you all the highlights of Bear Mountain." Hunter leaned forward, lowering his tone and putting every bit of his southern drawl into his voice. "Of course, if we're gonna be friends, I'd insist you call me Hunter."

Hunter thought he caught a ghost of a smile before her expression went blank. "I appreciate the offer, but right now, I need to concentrate on the job and not on making friends."

"But you're thinking about it, aren't you?" Maybe he was counting his chickens, but the brief flash of interest in her eyes couldn't have been all in his head, could it?

"I tell you what, Dr. Gracin. If I survive this week, I'll give your offer some thought." Flipping through a page in his file, she asked, "Now, do you have any other questions or concerns?"

Despite her all-business facade, Hunter wasn't deterred. In fact, he had a really good feeling that he and Ms. Fairchild were going to become *very* close.

Chapter 4

HUNTER STOOD ON the side of the OR table, searching for the bleeder in his patient's abdomen. Peter York, thirty-nine, had come in with a rigid abdomen, a concussion, and scrapes and bruises along his body after a nasty fall. His buddy had told his intake nurse that they'd been hiking, and Peter had been startled by a bear on the trail. Based on the man's camouflage duds from head to toe, Hunter suspected they were illegally hunting said bear, who had turned the tables on them. Not that it mattered; it wasn't Hunter's business what they were doing up on that mountain.

He just needed to make sure that Peter York made it off the table.

Finally, he found the source of the problem, and once he applied the clamps and suctioned, he could see exactly what needed to be done. As he removed Peter's spleen, he started humming an old Garth Brooks song. Hunter's cool demeanor and speedy hands were what had gotten him offers from several of the best trauma centers in the US, but Hunter had wanted to go where he was needed. And Bear Mountain had been in desperate need of an excellent trauma surgeon.

Sure, the equipment was outdated and some of the nurses were testier than a mama grizzly with cubs, but he saw more than his fair share of action.

Plus, living in the same town as his best friend, Dex Belmont, had its perks. They had met in the army and kept in touch long after they'd been discharged. With Hunter's family back in Texas, things would have been a lot lonelier without Dex. And as much as he loved his parents, things were better when he and his three older brothers put some distance between them.

Finally, Hunter was able to close up. The clear, steady beeping on the monitors told him that Peter York had a good chance of pulling through. Maybe Peter would even give up bear hunting for good.

After Hunter exited the OR and cleaned up, he passed Allison Fairchild's open office door and peeked in. She was bent over some paperwork, squinting, and even though she was chewing on a pencil like a beaver, he still thought she was the prettiest thing he'd ever seen.

And he was almost positive she was feeling him, too. He just needed to give her time to adjust to life in Bear Mountain.

Hunter found Peter's wife in the waiting area. Noting the wife's pallor, he insisted she stay seated as he sat down next to her.

"Mrs. York, I'm Dr. Gracin."

"Is Pete all right?" Her voice wobbled, and Hunter took her hands in his, squeezing them gently.

"I had to remove his spleen, and he had some serious internal bleeding, but barring further complications, your husband should pull through just fine. He looks pretty beat up, though, so I want you to be prepared for that."

Mrs. York squeezed his hands hard, tears streaming down her cheeks. "Thank you so much, Dr. Gracin."

Then, to Hunter's surprise, the trembling, mild-mannered Mrs. York turned to the man next to her and started raining blows across his head and shoulders. "You idiot! You almost got him killed!"

Hunter tried to intervene, but her little fists were too fast for him to grab. "Mrs. York, this is not the time—"

"Mary! I'm sorry. He wanted to come."

Hunter lowered his voice to a soothing tone. "It's all right. You don't need to do that to your husband's friend." Hunter didn't have a lot of experience consoling women, but her sniffles seemed to subside. As he tried to comfort Mrs. York, Allison chose that moment to walk by the waiting room, pause in the doorway, and stare at him.

Then, a smile stretched across her full lips, taking his breath away.

When she disappeared, Hunter wished he could extract himself and go after her, but he had to do his job.

What the hell did that smile mean?

* * *

Dex ordered another round the minute his best friend walked through the door of the Grizzly. The local pub had hardwood floors, cedar walls, oak countertops, and stools at the bar. It had the feel of a log cabin, complete with a big fireplace on the east wall. Locals usually avoided peak hours during tourist season, but after ten, out-of-towners went looking for livelier haunts than the laid-back Grizzly.

"Hey, buddy," Hunter said, taking the stool next to Dex. "How did things go with that new tenant?"

Dex's mouth thinned just thinking about Allie Fairchild and her ultimatum. "She's a pain in the ass. Told me she wasn't going to pay me any rent until I fixed up the place, since I'd misled her about its *condition*."

Hunter whistled. "And you went for that?"

"My first reaction was to tell her to hop back into her little Jetta and get the hell off my property, but to tell you the truth, she wasn't wrong in her reasoning."

"So you're really letting her squat in your cabin for weeks? Are you going to hire that contractor?"

"Hell, no, I'm not paying for something I can do myself. Little Miss Thang can enjoy her stay, because as soon as I get the place up to snuff, I'm going to renegotiate with a three-hundred-dollar rent increase."

Penelope Davis set their beers down, smiling widely at Hunter. "Hey there. How was work?"

"It was good, Penny, thanks." Hunter gave her his million-watt grin, and Dex almost gagged as Penny blushed. Ever since Hunter had moved to town, all the local women had started falling over themselves trying to catch his eye.

Not that there were very many. At least Penny was cute with her splash of freckles, bright blue eyes, and long dark-brown hair. Yet for some reason, Hunter didn't seem interested in her.

When Penny went down the bar to help another couple, Dex nudged Hunter with his shoulder. "She likes you."

"She's a kid," Hunter said.

"What are you talking about? She's got to be in her twenties."

"And I'm in my thirties, man. I'm looking for someone to settle down and have kids with, not a plaything."

Dex sat back on his stool, staring at Hunter in surprise. "When did this happen?"

"When I turned thirty-four and realized that I wanted to do something more with my time than drink with you. I want to meet someone, get married and have a couple kids. You know, the whole 'warm apple pie with a side of vanilla ice cream' kind of life."

Just thinking about that scenario made Dex break out in a cold sweat. He wasn't against marriage, but he had a lot more oats to sow before he took the plunge. And he was only a year younger than Hunter.

"Anyone in particular you've got your eye on, then?" Dex asked.

"As a matter of fact, I met our new director, Allison Fairchild, and she is stunning."

Dex choked on the swig of beer he'd just taken and barely managed to swallow before he had a loud coughing fit. Hunter slammed his hand between Dex's shoulder blades. "You okay, man?"

"Yeah, I'm good." Dex wheezed.

"Did you suck some down the wrong pipe or have you met her already?"

"*Allie's* my pain-in-the-ass tenant."

Hunter laughed. "Allie, huh? Small world." Suddenly, he sobered. "You're not interested, are you?"

Dex spluttered, "Hell, no! What gave you that idea?"

Throwing up his hand, Hunter said, "Whoa, I was just asking, man. Didn't want to piss in your patch."

"Believe me, my friend, the last thing I'm interested in is a difficult city girl who won't last the month here. You're welcome to her."

Chapter 5

TWO DAYS LATER, Allie was sitting at her desk staring down at the mountain of paperwork and invoices in front of her. The hospital needed so many updates, it seemed as if all she'd done since getting to Bear Mountain was sign checks.

The only bright spot in all the mundane tasks were the few times Hunter Gracin would walk by her open door with a smile or a wave. Not that she was looking for a boyfriend, but she'd be pretty well off with a guy like Hunter. He was successful, grounded, handsome, and nice, and much better than any other candidates she'd met.

Like Dex Belmont.

No, Dex wasn't even in the running. He was too cocky, he'd already proved he was a little shady, and he was totally the kind of guy who would love her and then leave her high and dry. She didn't need another jerk to rock her world; she needed a partner with his shit together.

It was why she needed to really think about every move she made here. Her past was filled with regrettable career choices, and a string of bad relationships. Her mother liked to throw them in her face whenever she mentioned Allie's two older, happily married sisters. Both had married men with impeccable New York pedigrees and were loaded to boot.

While Allie was happy her sisters had found love with men her parents approved of, Allie wanted more than what life had to offer in the city. She still wanted the right guy, which is why she started a checklist of all the qualities she was looking for in a man. Hunter matched it perfectly.

Dex, not so much.

Her desk phone rang, and she picked it up on the second ring. "Allison Fairchild."

"Hello, Ms. Fairchild," her assistant, Rebecca Kirkland, said. "If you still want to lend a hand, they're short a surgical nurse and have a family coming in with multiple injuries. Car accident."

Allie hesitated for a brief moment, taking in the mess she'd be leaving behind. But it would all be waiting when she got back in an hour or two.

"I'll be right down." Allie quickly shrugged out of her business casual attire and changed into the purple scrubs she kept in her desk drawer. With her stethoscope in hand, she ran for the stairs. When she finally burst into the emergency area, gurneys were being wheeled in, one after another. Hunter was directing people and Allie made her way toward him without even thinking about it. Maybe it was because he seemed to be the only one besides Rebecca who hadn't hated her on sight, or perhaps it was watching him with that patient's wife, but she liked him.

And it didn't hurt to make friends.

"Hey, I heard you needed some help down here," she said, coming up alongside him.

He glanced her way with a puzzled look. "I thought you were our administrator?"

"Well, I'm also a trauma nurse, and a pretty decent one, actually."

Hunter gave her a wide grin, his blue eyes dancing with amusement. "Is that a fact?"

"It is a fact, so if you can use me…"

"I can use you. Dex should be coming with another critical case any minute."

"Dex?"

Crap, please don't let it be—

The automatic doors opened and in rolled a gurney manned by two paramedics….

And her jerk of a landlord sitting astride the patient, administering chest compressions. Against her will, her gaze was drawn to those strong, corded arms as he pressed down hard with each compression, his face tight with concentration. Tiny beads of sweat gathered at his temples and she had the craziest urge to dab his forehead.

"What do we have?" Hunter asked.

Shaking herself, she slapped on her all-business face. Old habits die hard, but she was determined to focus on cute, reliable men like Hunter, and not dishonest, sneaky, hot, sexy men like…

"Fifty-six-year-old male, suspected heart attack," Dex said breathlessly. "He was unconscious in the field, and his pulse was weak and thready up until a minute ago—"

"Are you a paramedic?" Allie asked abruptly.

Dex paused in his compressions as he glanced her way, piercing her with those intense green eyes. "No."

"Then maybe you should get off our patient and let us take over."

Allie realized that she'd said the wrong thing the minute the air chilled around her. The two paramedics looked at her as if she were an insect, and even Hunter frowned at her.

Dex climbed off, and let one of the paramedics climb up. "Whatever the boss wants."

Damn it, she'd let her emotions get the better of her and acted like an elitist bitch. She'd wanted him gone, but she hadn't meant to sound so cutting.

"All right, Trauma Two, let's go," Hunter said.

As they rushed the man off, Allie hesitated, opening her mouth to apologize.

"Shouldn't you go with them? Make sure they're doing their job right?"

Allie's cheeks burned. Of course he probably thought she was some kind of tyrant, but she really wasn't. She had no idea what it was about Dex that made her want to prick him with every barb in her arsenal. She wasn't usually like this.

But she couldn't tell Dex any of that, because he was already walking out the door.

Pushing him from her mind, she hurried to Trauma Two and found the patient surrounded by Hunter and several nurses.

"We've got it covered," he called out, barely glancing at her while he charged the paddles. Then he yelled, "Clear."

His brush-off was so painful that Allie felt as if he had put the paddles to her. *So much for having one ally.*

Dex found his truck in the parking lot with Bluebell waiting patiently in the backseat. He'd asked Brian Darcy, one of Bear Mountain's firefighters, to follow behind the ambulance in it, and Dex was definitely thankful to live in a small town where people could be trusted. Where people knew him and his background.

Everyone except Allie.

Dex slammed his palm against the steering wheel, letting loose a string of curses that would have made his grandma blush. It had taken all of his self-control not to lay into Allie Fairchild and her snotty, condescending attitude, but he'd been the bigger man, turned the other cheek.

For all the good it did him. He knew he'd be stewing for days about this incident.

Bluebell leaned over the back of the seat and nuzzled his ear. It was the hound's attempt to calm him, but Dex was too fired up. It wasn't as if he didn't have any medical training, didn't know how to administer CPR, yet he'd let her treat him like an idiot.

He hated that. Growing up with parents like his hadn't been easy. He'd been an ordinary kid who preferred fishing to calculus, and their disapproval had given him a bit of an inferiority complex. He could admit that. And Miss High-and-Mighty New York Princess had hit the nerve like a dart to a bull's-eye.

The only reason he had been at the scene of the accident was that he was driving behind them when the car had swerved off the road and hit a tree. Dex stopped to check on them and found the husband unresponsive, with a weak heartbeat. The wife was crying in the front seat with a head wound, and their two teenagers were in the back with minor injuries. Dex called it in and started on the husband, which was probably what had kept him alive until the ambulance arrived.

But he couldn't tell Allie that or she might have thought he cared about her opinion of him. Which he didn't. At all.

Heading out toward the Bear Mountain Search and Rescue building, he cracked his neck and rolled his shoulders, trying to relieve some of the tension plaguing him.

Suddenly, something small and brown ran out in front of his truck. Swerving, he glanced back to see the little fur ball in the road, unhurt. Few cars came out this way, so Dex stopped and got out, making his way back toward the animal. He wasn't sure what it was until it lifted its head and he saw the floppy ears and long snout.

It was a puppy, and not a very old one by the looks of it. The dog cowered as Dex got closer, and started to slink away.

"Hey, buddy. It's okay." Dex kneeled down a few feet away and held out a hand. "I promise you'll be safe with me."

The puppy responded to his voice by submissively moving forward, and Dex saw the wet trail of urine it left behind. When it was finally within reach, Dex picked up the pup, noting its smelly, matted fur, and looked around. No one lived out this way, which made Dex suspect the little dude had been dumped in the forest.

Dex headed into the woods where the pup had come from, whistling, but there wasn't another sound. Fairly confident the pup was alone, he headed back to the truck and climbed into the driver's side, setting the pup on the passenger seat. Bluebell whined and tried to climb over the backseat, but a firm "Stay" from Dex had her sitting back, her long ears perked as she eyed the puppy.

And as the pup sat back, Dex got a good look at the little guy's stumpy left front paw. Dex couldn't tell what breed it was, but he had a feeling that its owners hadn't been pleased by the pup's deformity, most likely something it had been born with. But why let it live to be six, seven weeks before they dumped it?

Grabbing a blanket from the back, he tucked it around the little guy. "What do you say we get you a bath and some grub?"

The puppy cocked its head and whimpered.

Dex took that as a yes. Pleased to have something to focus on besides Allie Fairchild, he started up the truck and headed to work.

Chapter 6

IT WAS AFTER nine at night when Allie stumbled out of her office. She had put in a fourteen-hour day and she didn't just feel exhausted, she was also ready to get away from people. Since she'd made her snarky comment to Dex, the rest of the staff had been giving her a wide berth, including Hunter.

Speak of the devil, there he was, walking out the front door ahead of her. Allie picked up the pace, wanting to make peace with him.

"Excuse me, Dr. Gracin," she called, racing to catch up.

He paused just outside the entrance and waited for her. He was out of his scrubs and wearing a simple T-shirt and jeans. Jeez, were all the men in Bear Mountain immune to the cold? She was wearing wool tights under her slacks and still freezing her butt off.

"I am really sorry about earlier. Mr. Belmont is my landlord and we didn't exactly have the best first impression of each other, but that's no excuse for being rude and unprofessional.

I'll apologize to him, but I wanted you to know that behavior like that isn't normal for me."

Hunter crossed his arms over his chest. "I know Dex can be kind of a dick, pardon my French, but he's saved a lot of lives in this town. People respect him."

"Well, I'll do my best to get along with him and make things right." She gave Hunter a small smile and asked, "So what about you? 'Cause, to be honest, I need all the friends I can get."

"I suppose I could be persuaded to not join the angry mob…if you'll have a drink with me."

As much as she wanted to make amends, Allie was so tired that she'd rather get back to the cabin, crawl into bed, and sleep than try to be social tonight. "Can I take a rain check?"

"How about tomorrow? I have the day off; you have the day off. We could go exploring, maybe have a picnic before the weather gets too cold…."

"How do you know I have the day off?"

"I may have asked Rebecca if you were coming in."

Even when he was mad at her, he'd still asked about her schedule? How endearing was that? "Well…"

"I promise you'll have fun."

Think about the list. Plus, it would keep me away from the cabin so Dex can fix it.

Allie pictured being stuck in the cabin all day with Dex; sweaty, shirtless Dex in a tool belt and swinging a hammer with those strong arms….

"Okay, yeah. A picnic with a friend sounds great."

"For now," he said, grinning.

"What?"

"Friends for now."

Laughing softly, she shook her head. "I get the feeling you don't hear the word *no* a lot."

"Not often, but I promise I'll be the perfect gentleman. Would nine tomorrow morning work for you?"

"Nine is perfect," she said.

"And just to show what a swell guy I am, I'll walk you to your car."

"You know, most men don't call themselves 'swell' anymore."

"What can I say, I'm a throwback." Hunter put his hand on the small of her back, and the warmth of his palm was comforting. It made her feel safe and cared for, a feeling she could definitely get used to.

God knew none of the boyfriends she'd left behind had ever shown her such consideration. And as he took her keys and unlocked her door, she didn't feel the need to remind him she was more than capable of doing so herself.

When she pulled in front of the cabin fifteen minutes later, she glanced over at Dex's house and saw that the lights were still on inside.

Tomorrow morning I can talk to him. Tonight I have a date with my new flannel sheets.

Plus, Allie wanted to get a few more boxes unpacked before

bed. She climbed the porch steps and unlocked the front door. She flipped on the light and took one step inside when something big stood up on her counter, staring at her with black, beady eyes.

And she let out a bloodcurdling scream.

Chapter 7

DEX HAD JUST put Bluebell and the puppy into crates when he heard Allie's scream. Grabbing his rifle off the rack above the fireplace, he ran the hundred yards to the cabin, only to find Allie standing on the porch, holding the front doorknob, and shaking visibly.

"Are you all right?"

"There…there's an animal in the cabin!"

Dex brushed past her, opened the door and stepped inside. On top of the counter with a mangled box of crackers in its hands was a big, fat raccoon. The animal dropped down onto all fours and arched its back, letting out a high growl.

The door squeaked open behind him, and Allie hissed, "Shoot it!"

"I'm not going to shoot it."

"Then why the hell did you bring a gun?"

"In case." Dex glanced around, looking for any of the coon's buddies, but he seemed to be alone.

"Okay, seriously, there is a wild animal eating my brand-new box of Ritz crackers and you are standing there staring at it! Aren't you supposed to be a big, tough mountain man?"

Dex saw the tufts of fur at the edge of the hole in the ceiling. "Looks like he came in through the attic."

"Well, hallelujah, Sherlock, looks like you solved the mystery of how it got in. Now how about you get it the hell *out?*"

Dex sighed and pulled out his phone. Looking over his shoulder at her, he said mildly, "Just a little friendly advice, but the next time someone comes to your rescue, you might want to be a little more grateful."

"I would be grateful if you were actually helping!"

Dex dialed his buddy, Deputy Luke Teller, who picked up on the second ring. "Teller."

"Hey, it's Dex."

"What's up, man? I was getting ready to knock off."

"Before you do, I've got a raccoon situation in the cabin."

Luke sighed heavily into the phone. "Give me ten minutes."

Dex ended the call and guided Allie back out the door. "A deputy will be out in a few minutes to take care of your buddy there."

"You called the sheriff for a *raccoon?*"

Dex gritted his teeth. "I'm getting a little tired of you treating me like I'm an idiot."

"I don't understand why you can't shoo it or shoot it!"

"Because the sheriff's department, which doubles as our

animal control, can tranquilize him and relocate him, whereas if I shoot him, you're cleaning up the raccoon bits."

"Oh." Although it was dark on the porch, the kitchen light streaming from the front door highlighted her flushed cheeks. "I'm sorry."

"I appreciate the apology," Dex said, despite the fact that it hadn't done much to appease him. He also couldn't ignore the fact that Allie looked cold, if the arm-rubbing and shivers were any indication. "Why don't you come over to my place while you wait? At least it's warm in there. I'll look for something to cover up that hole until I can patch it in the morning."

She seemed to hesitate, so Dex shrugged. "Look, it's up to you. You can stay out here and wait in the cold or you can come sit by my fire." He walked down the porch steps, grinning as he called over his shoulder, "But fair warning: raccoons sometimes jump down from trees onto people's backs when they're feeling threatened. He could have friends watching you right now."

He heard her steps pick up behind him, and started whistling. Hey, he might be a gentleman, but that didn't make him a saint.

Chapter 8

ALLIE COULDN'T STOP shooting laser beams at the back of Dex's head as he walked into his big kitchen. She'd known he was probably messing with her about the raccoon jumping on her, but that hadn't stopped her skin from crawling. She had never been much of an outdoorsy person. The one time she'd gone away to camp, she'd begged her parents to come get her after one night, since she'd stayed up the whole time jumping at every noise.

"Are you hungry? I've got some leftover pasta. Or I can make some coffee."

"I'm already jittery, so I don't need to add caffeine. Thanks, though."

Allie sat down on the couch and studied the large open living room that bled into a beautiful kitchen. Everything was rustic, except for the stainless steel appliances. There were framed arrowheads on the walls, dozens of them, and the large fireplace roared with golden-red flames, casting dancing shadows on the cedar walls.

Dex came back in with two glasses of amber liquid and held one out to her. "Here, this will calm your nerves."

"What is it?" she asked.

"It's whisky. Don't tell me you're too good for whisky, too?"

His challenge had the desired effect, and she took the glass, downing the contents in one gulp. Her throat blazed as the liquid raced down, pooling warmly in her belly. Her eyes watered and she tried not to cough.

"Looks like I was wrong about you. You drink whisky like a champ," Dex teased, sitting on the couch across from her.

"What did you…ahem…what did you mean by I'm 'too good for whisky, too'?"

"Nothing. You don't seem to really fit in around here."

"Or maybe you have something against me because I don't fall at your feet—like every other woman—just because you're hot."

He quirked his left brow. "You think I'm hot, huh?"

"Don't get too full of yourself. Pretty is as pretty does. Just because you're nice to look at doesn't mean anything to me."

"Is that so?" He stood up and bent to take her glass, leaning in far closer than he needed to. His face was only a few inches from hers and she fought the urge to pull away, refusing to let him think he was getting to her. "So, what does affect you, Allie Fairchild?"

Allie's heart slammed against her breastbone as she stared into those bright-green eyes.

Your eyes. Your shoulders. That sneaky tattoo that continues to tease me…

The sound of a cage rattling and a whimper broke the spell.

"What is that?" she asked.

"That would be Kermit." Dex stood up, making it easier for her to breathe once more. He walked across the room and bent over, messing with something she couldn't see.

"What's a Kermit?"

He stood back up with a fluffy bundle of adorableness in his arms. "This is a Kermit."

Allie felt her heart liquefy into a gooey puddle as Dex brought the puppy closer. When he sat down next to her, she didn't even protest, she was so fixated on the sweetest face she'd ever seen.

"Aw, pumpkin, come here." Without asking, she took the puppy from Dex, snuggling him close to her chest. "You are so freaking cute. Where did he find you?"

"I found him this afternoon. Someone had dumped him, probably because he's got a deformed paw. He was a sad little pup at first, but after a couple of baths and some grub, he finally started to perk up."

Allie held the puppy out, studying the paw, and he scrambled to get close to her again, his little tongue darting out toward her. Laughing, she let him lick her nose and hugged him once more. "What kind of dog is he?"

"My best guess is a sheltie. He looks like a tiny Lassie, right?"

"He does." As Dex reached out and stroked Kermit's head, his hand brushed Allie's collarbone and they both stilled. Staring at each other over the puppy's head, she said, "It was good that you stopped. He might have died out there."

"I'd never leave an animal like that."

"Just like you wouldn't shoot the raccoon when you knew you could have him tranquilized and relocated."

Was it the fire finally warming her or had the temperature suddenly amped up?

"I told you, I didn't want the mess," he said softly.

"I don't believe you. I think underneath the dickish exterior, you're a big old softy."

Was she actually flirting with Dex?

Danger! Danger! Abort!

"That's what you think, huh?" He leaned a little closer, and whether it was the lull of his voice or the whisky clouding her judgment, she did the same.

"Yeah. Am I wrong?"

His lips were so close and he smelled so good that she licked her own.

"Absolutely."

Allie closed her eyes, anticipation humming through her body....

The loud pounding on the front door made her jerk back, and his hound started baying.

Dex sat back, his expression unreadable. "That would be Luke."

Realizing what almost happened, Allie moved away from Dex on the couch. "You should probably get that."

He stood up without another word and went to grab the door. Meanwhile, Allie kissed Kermit on the head, cursing herself. *That's it. No more whisky. No more raccoons. And definitely no more alone time with Dex Belmont.*

Chapter 9

DEX WALKED OUT of the cabin with Luke, grimly. By the time they'd gone back inside Allie's home, the raccoon was gone. They'd boarded up the hole with a piece of cardboard, but it was only a temporary fix. If the raccoons really wanted in, they could do it with very little effort.

Which meant that Dex either needed to repair it tonight or let Allie stay in his guest room and come over to take care of it in the morning.

Or she could just share my bed.

No, that was a bad idea. He couldn't get involved with her, especially after what Hunter had said the other night. It was one thing to have a casual thing with his tenant—that'd be wrong in itself—but to screw over his best friend?

He wasn't that much of an asshole.

After Luke left, Dex made his way back to his place and found Allie on the floor of his living room, playing with Kermit. When she looked up at him, he forgot for a second that Hunter had called dibs and she wasn't meant for him.

What he really wanted to do was cross the room and kiss her, just to see what she tasted like.

"Did he get it?" she asked.

"No, it was gone and will probably be back, especially now that it knows there's food inside. So I can set up the spare bedroom for you and fix the—"

"You...you want me to stay here tonight? With you?" Shaking her head, she said, "I don't think that's a good idea."

"Look, it's not as if I'm going to sneak into bed with you. It's late and it seems like the simplest solution."

"I think I'll take option two and go back to the cabin. You covered the hole, right? It probably won't come back tonight, anyway."

Dex didn't know whether to be exasperated or exhausted. "You would rather sleep in the cabin and risk another animal encounter than stay in my very comfortable guest room?"

"Yes, I think I would." She stood up with Kermit in her arms. "What are your plans for this guy?"

"I don't have any yet, besides getting him in to see the vet—"

"So if I wanted to adopt him that would be okay with you?"

"Aren't you gone all the time?" Dex asked.

"I can find a pet sitter to watch him while I'm at work."

Dex couldn't say it was a bad idea. Allie did seem taken with him. "He needs his shots."

"I'll get them. I promise, he'll be in good hands."

Unable to come up with a reason to say no, Dex grabbed the crate he'd set up for Kermit and nodded toward the door. "I'll walk you back and get him set up."

"Thank you. I'll return it when I get my own." They walked outside and Allie paused. "Thanks for everything tonight, too. I may have misjudged you."

As they crossed the yard toward the cabin, he shot her a wolfish grin. "You mean I'm not a conniving liar who has no business getting in the way of professionals?"

"Yet another apology I meant to give you. I am sorry I was so horrible at the hospital. I'm not usually like that, it's just—"

"I get it, you don't like me and I was stepping on your turf."

"I'm not territorial and I didn't say I didn't like you!"

He reached past her to open the cabin door, and their chests brushed. Allie sucked in a harsh breath, and when his gaze dropped to her parted lips, it took every ounce of willpower not to do it. Not to give in and press her up against the door and kiss her until she was begging for more.

Of course, with Kermit in her arms like a furry shield, it would be a little hard to do, but if he really wanted to, he could probably manage it.

"So you're saying you do like me?"

"I'm saying that everyone deserves another chance at a first impression." She moved past him, leaving him to watch her hips swing as she walked into the kitchen.

"That's mighty nice of you."

Damn, she made a power suit hot.

He saw her face fall as she surveyed the damage. "It's going to take me hours to clean this up."

"Tell you what. Let's get Kermit set up, and then I'll help you."

"Well, I suppose that's only fair, since it's your fault it got inside in the first place," she said teasingly.

"You know, a simple 'thank you' would work."

"Just speaking the truth."

Dex followed her into her bedroom and set the crate down, surveying the changes she'd already made to the room. A set of blackout curtains covered the window, and across the dresser were a couple of picture frames. One of an older couple, and another with Allie hugging two other women who looked so much like her they had to be her sisters.

Dex almost asked about it, but figured it was none of his business.

Pulling out the bowl of food and water bowl that had spilled a bit in transport, he said, "He might need a dry towel or something."

"I'll take care of it."

Dex left her bedroom, the image of Allie curled up under her black-and-white bedspread too tempting by half.

Dex got to work on the kitchen, and a few minutes later, Allie walked in. "You know, you're probably tired. I can finish up."

"I don't mind. Besides, I thought this was my fault," he said.

"I just…I want to be clear that we need to keep things between us cordial. You're my landlord—"

"Actually, a landlord gets paid."

Frustration marred her pretty face, and she seemed to be clenching her jaw. "Be that as it may, I'm not looking for complicated. And I feel like if anything develops between us it will be just that."

Why her assumption bothered Dex, he couldn't guess. He deliberately brushed every last bit of cracker into the trash and came around the counter. Standing in front of her, he said, "Actually, things with me would be pretty simple, sweetheart. We'd have fun until one of us got bored and we'd say good-bye. Nothing complicated about that."

Dex saw a flash of something in the brown depths of her eyes. Temptation? Whatever it was, it was gone as soon as it appeared and her expression became hard as steel.

"Well, I'm not in the market for that, either. I need to get settled in and concentrate on work. Nothing more."

His lips a hairsbreadth away from hers, he whispered, "Your loss."

Before she smacked him, he turned and headed for the door. Pausing with his hand on the knob, he had to get the last word in.

"But just so you know, winter is coming and it can get mighty cold round here. If you change your mind and need some warming up, you know where I'll be."

Chapter 10

ALLIE WOKE UP to the sun barely streaming into her bedroom. Hadn't she closed those damn curtains last night? Kermit was whining, probably because he needed to go potty and was tired of being in his crate, so Allie swung her legs off the side of the bed. Her clock on the nightstand read six-thirty in the morning, and for the briefest moment, she wondered what had possessed her to ask for the dog. Now she was going to have to take him outside at all hours while she housetrained him.

Groaning, she opened his crate and picked him up. The minute his little body snuggled against her, the grumpiness melted away.

"What do you say we take you to go potty and have a bowl of cereal?"

A tiny, excited tongue on her chin was her answer as she opened the bedroom door and made her way to the living room. She set him down briefly to pull on her jacket and her boots by the back door, sweeping him into her arms before he got the chance to have an accident. Taking him out the side door, she shivered as the cool morning air bit through her thin pajama pants. She was really going to need to invest in a flannel set and some house slippers. She walked down the back porch steps and let Kermit down.

"Go ahead, pumpkin."

The puppy nosed around at the dirt and leaves for a few seconds before he squatted down to do his business. Allie's gaze wandered around the forest, grudgingly admitting that it was a beautiful place. She could get used to being here.

When Kermit was done, Allie called him over and picked him up. Once they were back inside, she set him down on the hardwood floor and took off her boots and outerwear once more.

"What do you think? Kibble for you, Fruity Pebbles for me?"

Kermit chased after her feet, skidding across the floor when she stopped abruptly once she saw the kitchen.

As she took in the chaos of the crime scene with horror, Allie's emotions twisted between fear and fury. She looked up at the cardboard covering the hole in the ceiling, but it was still in place. How the hell had that furry bastard gotten back in last night? Then her gaze landed on her box of Fruity Pebbles, which had been snug and safe in the cupboard when she'd gone to bed. The cupboard that now hung wide open, like a giant mocking mouth.

Her delicious Fruity Pebbles. The box had been ripped open and its guts shredded. What was left of the colorful cereal was spread across the counter and smashed into what looked suspiciously like raccoon feces.

Allie's entire body surged with molten rage.

"Damn you, you no-good son of a bitch!" Allie threw the chewed-up box of cereal across the room, surprised when she heard a familiar grunt.

She looked up toward her front door and found Dex standing in the doorway. He stooped to pick up the mangled box, giving her a dry look as he tossed it onto the overturned trash can.

"I've been dreaming my whole life about a woman who looks like an angel and cusses like a sailor."

Allie glanced around for something else to throw, but couldn't find anything worthwhile.

"What is it with you? Don't you know that cheesy lines and breaking and entering are *not* sexy?"

The panty-melting grin he shot her almost made a liar out of her. "That's too bad, 'cause that's all the game I've got."

"Obviously! What are you even doing here this early?"

Waving at the tool belt on his hips, he said, "I have the day off, so I figured I'd get started on those repairs. After all, the sooner I get them done, the sooner you start paying me."

"Next time, you need to call and then knock before you just come barging in. I could have been sleeping or in the shower."

"Now you're just teasing me," he said, shamelessly grinning at her.

"Whatever. The first thing you can do is figure out how he got in because your stupid cardboard is still there."

Dex walked over to stand under the cardboard, turning his head from every angle, as if looking for a weakness. "Huh. Maybe he never left the cabin after all. Maybe he's in a cupboard or something right now?"

Allie picked up Kermit, her gaze darting around the room in alarm. "Do you think so?"

"Could be. I'll do a thorough search. Your cupboards, your closets…I should probably check your underwear drawer, too."

She realized he was messing with her, again, and glared at him. "Ha-ha, I had my door shut, so there's no way he was in my room." A lump crawled up her throat, and she hated that she was about to cry, especially in front of Dex. "Please just find him and make sure he doesn't get in again, okay? I can't stand the thought that he might hurt Kermit if I don't realize he's in here."

Every trace of humor left his face. "I'll fix the problem."

"Thank you." Grimly surveying the mess once more, she said, "I guess I'll put Kermit in his crate while I clean up."

Kermit wasn't happy about being locked up again, but she didn't want him underfoot while she cleaned. Especially if any raccoon poop had gotten onto the floor.

As she scrubbed the counter, her gaze kept straying to Dex as he inspected every nook and cranny. He looked good in the white T-shirt and jeans, the tool belt slung low on his hips. He was wearing a dark ball cap that covered his sun-streaked brown hair, and the shadow of the bill gave his face a mysterious edge.

Hunter. Focus on Hunter, remember? He's the catch here.

"I'll be gone most of the day, so don't worry about me being in your way."

"Working today?" he asked without turning around.

"No, Hunter Gracin is showing me around."

Did his shoulders stiffen or was that just her imagination?

"Oh, well, that'll be good. Hunter's a good guy."

"Yeah, he seems nice."

"Plus, he's a doctor."

Allie bristled at his tone, as if he were insinuating that was the only reason she'd said yes to Hunter. Okay, so he was settled with a career and that was a factor in her decision to go for him, but that didn't mean she was a gold digger. She had money of her own.

"What are you saying?"

"Nothing, I just know that most women want to score a man with money and a high-powered job. Doctors are the ideal, right?"

"I told you, I'm not looking for anything right now. Hunter and I are just friends."

He stood up with his hands in the air. "Whoa, don't jump all over me, sweetheart. I was making conversation. You don't have to explain yourself to me."

"I wasn't explaining myself, I was emphasizing the fact that there is nothing going on with Hunter!"

"Gotcha."

Allie violently tackled the rest of the cleanup, sanitizing the counter. Finally, she announced, "I'm going to take a shower."

The jerk had the nerve to leer at her. "You telling me 'cause you want some company?"

That was enough. Grabbing an apple from the bowl, she hurled it at Dex's head. He barely ducked out of the way in time, but when the edge of the apple skimmed his shoulder, she felt marginally better.

Until she reached the door to the bedroom and she heard him shout, "You've got some weird ideas about foreplay, darling."

Slamming the door closed and locking it with a click, Allie threw herself across the bed and buried her head in the pillow before releasing a frustrated scream.

Chapter 11

HUNTER CLIMBED THE steps to Allie's cabin and knocked on the door. It was five minutes to nine, and he was really hoping that she wasn't one of those women who are chronically late.

The door swung open and Dex stared out at him, a hammer in his hand.

"What's up, buddy?"

Hunter arched a brow at him as he stepped inside. "It's awfully early to be working on repairs, isn't it?"

"There was a raccoon invasion last night, so I am being a good landlord and dealing with the issue."

"I thought she wasn't paying you."

"She's not, but she will be soon."

"Hi," Allie said, coming into the kitchen with a puppy in her arms. She was decked out in leather boots, tight blue jeans, and a blue long-sleeved top. Her golden-blond hair fell around her shoulders in loose waves and he was struck again by how pretty she was.

For some reason, Hunter glanced toward Dex, and he stiffened as he recognized his friend's expression.

Hunger.

Dex had been adamant about having no interest in Allie, but…as Hunter took a long time to process everything that was happening around him, he decided that Dex was simply looking at Allie the way he did every beautiful woman.

Relaxing, Hunter stepped forward and kissed Allie's cheek. "You look amazing." Taking the puppy from her arms, he held him up until he was at eye level. "And who's this handsome dude?"

"This is Kermit. Dex found him yesterday and I am keeping him. Isn't he adorable?"

"Real men don't say adorable," Dex grumbled, but Hunter heard him.

"Oh, he's definitely adorable." He waited for Dex to give him shit, but his friend silently climbed the ladder under the hole in the ceiling, ignoring him. "I figured we'd start off by taking a drive around town, and I can show you all the places I love around here. Then we'll stop for a picnic.

"Then I was thinking later we'd go by the Grizzly and have dinner," Hunter said. "So is it all right if we put Kermit in his cage tonight? You're not really living until you've had a pulled pork sandwich and a frothy mug of BearFaced Brown."

"I'm afraid to ask what that is," Allie said.

"It's this awesome potato ale made in Idaho, by the Bear Island Brewing Company. It's tasty, you'll like it."

"I'm in."

"Is it cool if you watch Allie's pup for now, Dex?"

Dex grunted, and Hunter called up again, "You okay?"

"Fine. Why don't you two get the hell out of here so I can work in peace?"

Something had definitely crawled up Dex's ass and died there, but Hunter wasn't going to pry it out of him now. Allie grabbed her jacket, a hat, and gloves and gave Dex a withering look.

After going to the front door, Hunter held it open and waved Allie through.

Once she was outside, he shot one more glance at Dex, who finally looked his way.

"What the hell, man?" Hunter mouthed.

Dex didn't answer him, just went back to hammering. Shaking his head, Hunter closed the door with a *thump*.

Dex slammed the hammer down on his thumb for the third time in an hour and hollered. "Shit!" Throwing the hammer down, he climbed off the ladder and wished that he had something to swing at. He had no idea what had set his teeth and temper on edge, but he was pretty sure the blame sat at Allie Fairchild's sweet little booted feet.

Dex could chalk it up to the feeling of wanting what he couldn't have, but there had been women in the past he'd backed off of for a friend and been happy to. And seeing Allie look so relaxed, with her hair soft and touchable, had thrown him. Especially when he started imagining Hunter running his fingers through it.

She's just one woman. A woman who doesn't even think you're good enough for her, anyway.

The voice in his head was right, of course. What he needed was to keep his mind focused on someone else.

Pulling his phone out of his pocket, he scrolled through his contacts, finally landing on Iris Jacobs, a recent divorcée with a wild streak a mile long.

And his finger hovered over the Call button.

After exploring Bear Mountain for several hours, Allie and Hunter sat at the base of a mountain, eating their picnic lunch. A river bubbled and broke fifty feet away, and the view of statuesque mountains and pine trees was beautiful. The sun was out, and warmed the air slightly, but Allie still kept her coat on. So far, the date had been going very well. Hunter was funny, charming, and a gentleman.

"I found this spot when I was out driving and, I don't know, it just became my place. I haven't brought anyone else up here."

Hunter's words were romantic and right. They were sharing a lovely picnic and the sounds of rushing water from a river nearby were positively soothing.

So why didn't her heart flutter the way it had when Dex had stared at her this morning?

I need to put that man from my mind for one afternoon. Why is that so hard?

"Well, I'm honored," she said.

"If you want to feel even more honored, grab a brownie from the basket. I know it's not manly, but baking is actually the one thing I can do outside of the OR on rare occasions."

"You bake?" A man who was gorgeous, successful, and baked? Hunter was beyond the total package.

Allie grabbed one of the brownies and took a bite with relish. "Mmmm, seriously, you should patent these bad boys."

"That would require sharing my great-grandmother's recipe, which would be a mortal sin," Hunter said.

Allie popped the rest of the moist, chewy goodness in her mouth, humming with pleasure.

"Uh-oh, I forgot to pack something," he said.

Trying to swallow the chewy bite, she took a drink from her water bottle. "What?"

"Napkins." He scooted closer. "And you've got something right"—he reached up and trailed his finger over her lips—"there."

Allie knew what was about to happen before his lips closed over hers, brushing and tasting her softly, as if he was savoring her. Allie kissed him back, opening her mouth to his tongue.

The sound of something screeching overhead brought Allie scrambling away and glancing up toward the sky.

"What the heck was that?"

"I didn't hear anything," Hunter said.

Allie's cheeks warmed at the insinuation. He hadn't heard anything because he'd been too busy kissing her, while she…

She'd been distracted by a bird.

It wasn't that Hunter wasn't a good kisser; he was. There just wasn't any…

Spark.

Yet. She couldn't judge Hunter based on her experiences in her past relationships. Those had been crazy hot in the beginning, but fizzled out quickly. She wanted something that was going to last.

"Sorry, I'm not used to the great outdoors."

Hunter, easygoing and nice, just smiled. "Don't worry about it."

Allie figured she'd blown it after that, especially since he started packing up their food. But after he picked up the basket, he took her free hand and held it all the way to the car. Even opened the door for her and gave her a sweet, chaste peck before closing her door.

Everything was perfect about their date, and yet, she wanted to roll her eyes.

Chapter 12

DEX ORDERED ANOTHER drink for Iris, some fruity cocktail with a ridiculous name, and another whisky for him. He'd downed three already, but who could blame him? He'd forgotten how grating Iris's nasal voice was.

He pretended to listen to Iris bitch about how cheap her ex was, nodding and grunting as he looked past her shoulder toward the door.

I should have taken Iris somewhere else.

Except Dex hadn't wanted to go anywhere else, and if he was being honest with himself, it was because he wanted to see how Hunter and Allie's date had gone.

"I decided not to speak to him except through our attorneys. It's better for my stress level that way," Iris said.

"Makes sense," Dex said distractedly.

Iris's hand landed on his knee, moving its way up his jeans-clad thigh, indecently close to his crotch. "Here I am dominating the conversation with my complaining. My ex has the kids this weekend. Maybe we could go back to my place and I'll make it up to *you*."

Dex opened his mouth to answer, but the door swung open, and in stepped Hunter and Allie, both smiling and looking nauseatingly happy.

Until Allie's pretty brown eyes landed on him at the bar with Iris's hand in his lap, and her face crumpled into an unhappy scowl.

Was that look because he was there or because he was with Iris? Suddenly, Dex grinned, feeling better than he had all day. He climbed to his feet. "What do you say we play some pool, darling?"

Hunter and Allie had barely sat down at the bar when Penny walked over to take their order.

"What will it be?" she asked curtly.

Hunter, a little surprised by her attitude, asked, "You okay, Penny?"

"I'm fine, just busy."

Hunter glanced around at the handful of patrons in the bar, and as if following his line of thinking, Penny snapped, "I'm trying to study for my test, okay?"

"What kind of test are you taking?" Allie asked.

Penny seemed to hesitate before answering. "Animal biology. I'm going for my master's in zoology."

"That is amazing. I love animals. I just adopted a puppy that Dex Belmont found abandoned on the highway."

Penny's guarded expression flashed into one of outrage. "God, I hate people! Is the puppy okay?"

"Yeah, except he's got a lucky fin, like Nemo."

Penny's whole face melted into a soft, sweet smile. "Aw, poor sweetheart."

"You know, I need to find a pet sitter for him. I'm at the hospital during the day and I don't want him to get lonely or backtrack on his house-training. I was going to put a flyer up at the vet's office, but maybe—"

"I'll totally watch him," Penny said.

Hunter stared between the two women as they went back and forth, totally ignoring him as they ironed out the details of Kermit's new schedule. His gaze wandered to where Dex was, talking to a few bikers playing pool. Hunter shook his head and stood up. "I'll be right back. I'm gonna go say hi to Dex."

He noted Allie's dark look as she glanced toward his friend. "Okay."

If things continued between Allie and him, he was going to have to deal with the dislike between the two. He couldn't have his girl and his best friend hating each other.

Stopping beside the pool table, Hunter saw that Dex was concentrating hard on his next shot. It wasn't as if Dex couldn't handle himself when it came to hustling pool, but Hunter could already tell he'd had a bit to drink. And these guys didn't look like the type to take losing or Dex's good-natured ribbing well.

"Hey, buddy, what are you doing?"

Dex looked up from his shot. "What does it look like? I'm about to kick this guy's ass at pool."

Iris giggled nervously while the biker holding the pool cue didn't appear amused.

Dex took his shot, knocking two into the pockets, and stood up. Pulling his wallet out and holding some money out to Iris, he said, "Why don't you get us a few more drinks, honey? This won't take long."

Hunter shook his head and moved next to Dex. "Are you trying to get yourself killed? You don't know these guys and—"

"Dude, I'm fine. Why don't you go back to your date and see if you can pull that stick out of her ass?"

It took everything in Hunter not to slam his fist in Dex's jaw. "You're being a real asshole, man."

Dex lined up another shot, not even bothering to look at Hunter again. "Then maybe you should walk away."

Hunter did just that, heading back over to where Allie was watching him, her face a mask of concern as he sat down. "Everything okay?"

"Yeah, it's fine. He's like that sometimes. Whatever it is, he'll get over it."

Drunk or not, Dex was kicking the biker's ass, all right, and the dude did not look happy about it. Neither did his scruffy friend who was leaning against the wall, his arms crossed and bulging.

"Eight ball, corner pocket."

Dex took his shot, and as the ball sank in, both men cursed a blue streak while Iris, who had started to look a little bored two games ago, cheered loudly.

Dex grabbed the money off the side of the pool table, now a couple hundred deep, and slipped it into his pocket.

"I want to thank you, gentlemen, for such a splendid night—"

The biker who had lost, a mean-looking son of a bitch with a shaved head and a long, bushy beard, grabbed the front of Dex's shirt and pulled him forward. His face mere inches from Dex, he snarled. The dude's breath made Dex's stomach turn. "Where the hell do you think you're going? You aren't leaving until we have a chance to win our money back."

Dex smirked, too buzzed to recognize the danger he was in. Or maybe he'd just been spoiling for a fight. "I gave you three chances to win it back. Really, man, you oughta quit before I really clean you out."

Baldy didn't like that. He pulled back his burly arm to swing.

Dex ducked, ripping his shirt, and swung, nailing the guy in the gut with his fist. Dex weaved a bit, off-balance, as Baldy stumbled back against a table.

Suddenly, Baldy's friend was there, shoving Dex. He fell backward, hitting the floor so hard it knocked the wind out of him.

Dex tried to get his bearing back just as another biker stepped forward with a pool cue raised over his head.

"Ah, hell!"

Allie stopped talking at Hunter's exclamation and was left alone and dumbfounded as he jumped up and raced across the room. Allie spun around and saw Dex on the ground. One of the men he'd been playing pool with stood over him, a pool stick in his hand. Allie's gut lurched as she realized he was about to hit Dex with it.

Hunter got there as the man was bringing it down, and grabbed the pool cue out of the biker's hand. He threw it across the room. Allie hollered a warning as the other biker made a move at Hunter's back.

And then Dex was on his feet once again.

"Climb behind the bar!" Penny yelled, hopping over it with a baseball bat in hand.

"What the hell are you doing?"

"Squashing this shit," Penny said, tossing Allie a saucy grin before jumping into the fray.

Suddenly, a chair went whizzing through the air…right toward Allie's head. She barely had time to duck before it crashed into the bar wall behind her. Landing on the floor, she climbed back to her feet in time to watch Penny hit the biker attacking Hunter with her bat.

The rest of the bar was clearing out, including the woman who'd had her hand buried in Dex's lap when Allie had first walked in with Hunter. She'd tried not to let it bother her, but still…

Allie saw Dex being thrown over the pool table, the biker looming over him with his hands around Dex's neck. Hunter and Penny were busy pinning the other guy to the floor.

Allie had no idea what she was about to do, she only knew that she was running. She came up behind the biker and let her foot fly up from behind….

And it connected, hard, against his testicles.

The guy let out a high-pitched cry as he released Dex and fell to his knees, his back still to her. Allie hopped on one foot and nearly burst into tears as the pain in her foot radiated upward. As it subsided, Dex sat up coughing and wheezing, and their gazes locked. The light in his eyes when he looked at her stirred a warm, fuzzy glow in her chest, and she smiled at him through the pain.

And then the biker turned on her, looking seriously pissed off. "You stupid bitch."

As he took a step toward her, Allie realized that she should have taken Penny's advice and hidden behind the bar.

Chapter 13

DEX DIDN'T THINK as he launched himself onto the man's back, slipping his arm around his neck in a choke hold. He'd seen Allie's look of terror and lost all reason, jerking back hard as the guy clawed at his arm. The biker outweighed him by a good fifty pounds, but as Dex felt him start to go limp, he tossed him away from Allie as if he weighed nothing.

Then Dex was on him, throwing his fists until someone jerked him off the guy. Dex took in the blood oozing from Baldy's nose and lips, and his muscles relaxed.

"I'm okay, I'm fine."

Hunter released him and faced him with a look of rage. "What the hell were you thinking? The cops are on their way here and you're hammered. You can't drive—"

"I'll take him home," Allie said softly.

Dex glanced her way as Hunter tried to argue. "You don't have to do that."

"We're going to the same place. It's not as if I'm going out of my way or anything."

They were all standing around, talking about Dex as if he weren't there, and it was starting to piss him off.

Hunter nodded. "Okay, thanks. Dex, give Allie your keys."

Dex fished out his keys and handed them to Allie. Unfortunately, he didn't have time to turn away before Hunter stepped into her, gave her a kiss on the cheek, and said, "Sorry for the way our date ended."

"It's all right. I had fun until about ten minutes ago."

"So, you're saying getting into a bar fight wasn't on your bucket list?" Hunter asked jokingly.

"Yeah, not so much."

Hunter took Allie's hand, threading his fingers with hers. "Next time, we'll just stick to the fun."

Jealousy churned in Dex's stomach. He'd had enough. "If we're going, can we get a move on? I don't really want to spend the night in a cell with these two dickheads."

Both Allie and Hunter shot him a dirty look, but he was beyond caring. His head, his face, and his back…every part of him hurt and the room was starting to spin. The last thing he wanted to do was pass out at the Grizzly.

Finally, Allie released Hunter's hand and stepped forward, putting her arm around Dex's waist. "Come on."

Dex wrapped his arm around her shoulder and leaned on her a little more than he needed to.

*   *   *

Hunter roughly helped the bikers to their feet. He was already pissed about not being able to take Allie home, and now he was stuck here, cleaning up Dex's mess.

Come on, the last thing Dex needs is an assault charge on his record. Allie taking him home was the best option.

Still, Dex hadn't deserved the help tonight. He'd been an asshole this morning and in the hour before the fight broke out. For a moment or two, Hunter had gotten the feeling he was jealous of Hunter being out with Allie.

Trying to push his suspicions aside, Hunter stared into one of the burly biker's dark eyes.

"I'm going to go out on a limb and guess that your records aren't so clean that you can afford another run-in with the cops, so I'm giving you a chance. You can leave town now, no hard feelings, but if you stick around—"

"We're gone," one of the bikers said, shooting his buddies a warning glance. The guy who'd started it with Dex didn't look happy about it, but wasn't going to be stupid.

Once the bikers were out of the bar, Hunter handed Penny Dex's wallet. "This is Dex's. Whatever cash you find, give it to the owner. Dex will come in and work it out for the rest."

"And what about the other damages? Those men caused some, and so did you. Is Dex supposed to get stuck with the whole thing?" Penny asked.

Why is Penny being so hostile?

For some reason, Hunter was furious enough at Dex to

almost say yes, but he didn't. "No, I'll settle my part of the damages, too."

"Fine." Penny set the bat down on the bar and grabbed the broom. When she tossed it at him, he caught it in midair. "Then you can start now by helping me clean up this mess."

Allie parked Dex's truck in front of his place, ready to tell him to get out. He hadn't said a word to her the entire drive, which had left her alone with her thoughts and a roller-coaster of emotion.

I was just in a bar fight. A man came at me and Dex stopped him.

Allie opened her door and glanced over at Dex. A bruise was already discoloring his cheek, and the cuts and scrapes across his knuckles were probably going to be sore tomorrow. He looked so peaceful and beautiful despite his injuries. His lips, which had escaped unscathed...she was tempted to lean over and wake him up with a kiss.

Of gratitude, of course. For protecting her.

She needed to stop thinking like that. It was insane. The man was drunk as a skunk and beat up. She needed him to get moving, because there was no way she was going to carry him inside.

"Dex, wake up."

He snorted.

After she got out and went around to the passenger side, she pulled his door open and leaned in. Giving his shoulder a gentle shake, she hissed, "Dex, come on, you're gonna have to walk."

Grabbing his arm and putting it around her shoulder, she grunted as she tried to lift him out of the car.

"What are you trying to do, rip my arm off?" Dex mumbled.

"Yes, that is exactly what I'm trying to do, you idiot. I need your help. I can't carry you inside, so you're gonna have to stand up and walk."

"Whoa, why so snippy?" Dex stood up and leaned so hard against her she nearly stumbled.

"Will you at least try to walk straight? You're a lot bigger than me, and if you don't stop swaying, we're both going down."

They paused at the door, and while Allie searched through his key ring for the house key, she felt his breath rustle the top of her hair. "Is that an invitation?"

As his meaning sunk in, her head flew up and both of them cried out when her temple connected with his chin.

"Ow. No, that was not an invitation, you pervert."

"Why am I a pervert? You say something like that, what am I supposed to think?"

Finally, she found a key that worked. "I was trying to find this so I could get you inside instead of leaving you on your porch."

The man actually pouted at her. "You're cranky."

Allie counted to five, trying to find her patience. As she

unlocked the door, both of Dex's arms wrapped around her shoulders from behind and he leaned against her, his face buried in her hair. Her skin tingled at his proximity, and she told herself she didn't like it—loathed it, actually—but she couldn't deny that the feel of Dex's hard, lean body pressed against her back made her heart skip with excitement.

"You smell so good. Why do you have to smell so good?"

God, he was practically moaning against the back of her neck, and her hands began to tremble.

"I guess I could try not bathing," she said, trying to lighten the mood.

"Hmm, but you'd still be you."

What the hell did that mean?

Bluebell bellowed. Allie shuffled across the living room, Dex still hanging on to her.

"Where's your bedroom?"

"End of the hallway." His speech was really beginning to slur and Allie, afraid he was going to pass out on her, picked up the pace. Opening his bedroom door, she angled him toward the bed and loosened his arms.

"Here you go, big guy."

Dex flopped across the bed, the back of his head hitting the pillow with a groan. Allie lifted first one foot and then the other, untying his boots and dropping them to the floor. Then she placed his feet on the bed and moved up, trying to get him to lie straight.

While she leaned over him, his hand shot up, cupping

the back of her neck. Before she could make a sound, he'd brought her down and his soft, full lips met hers, moving coaxingly. Her mouth parted instinctively. The kiss was over too fast for her to fully process it, but as he flopped back on the bed, he mumbled something.

"What is it, Dex?" God, why did her voice have to sound so husky?

Louder, this time, she heard him. "You taste better."

Better? Better than what?

But before she could ask him, he let out a deep snore.

Chapter 14

A LITTLE OVER a week later, Allie flopped into her office chair with a moan. It felt as though she'd been running around nonstop, and her sensible heels had become torture devices. Kicking them off under her desk, she cracked her toes and flexed the arches, wincing at her sore muscles.

Every inch of her hurt, and while some of it was from being on her feet to oversee the hospital updates, most of it was due to stress.

For the last week, she'd been out with Hunter three more times. They'd gone to a movie, and grabbed dinner twice. He was the perfect gentleman and she liked him a lot.

But she just couldn't stop obsessing about the things Dex had said to her. Or that kiss, which she'd replayed again and again. It was so quick she'd hardly had time to realize what was happening, so why couldn't she forget it?

Not that she'd seen much of Dex since then. Either he remembered everything and had been avoiding her, or he had just been feeling lazy these days. He didn't start work on the cabin until she was gone, and he was never there when she arrived home. Still, he'd gotten the railing up on the front porch and there had been no more raccoons terrorizing her kitchen. She had to give it to him; every time she came home, the cabin looked better than when she'd left.

"How's my favorite hospital administrator?"

At the sound of Hunter's voice, Allie smiled warmly. She couldn't help it. She genuinely liked him.

"Fine. A little tired and my feet are killing me."

Hunter sat down in the other office chair and scooted around until he was next to her. He picked up one of her feet and held it in his lap.

And then, with the pad of his thumb, he pressed into the arch of her foot and started rubbing away all the aches.

Allie melted into her chair, whimpering with every squeeze, every press of his hands.

"Does that hurt?"

"In the best way possible," she said huskily.

For several more moments he continued massaging her feet, and then, suddenly, he was pulling her toward him so her legs straddled him on either side of his chair. Her eyes flew open as her simple black pencil skirt rode up her thighs. His arm wrapped around her waist and he dipped his head toward her lips.

"Someone could come in," she protested.

"I locked the door."

Such a bold move was surprising from Hunter, and as he

gave her a hard, passionate kiss, Allie had to admit that it did stir something inside her. But was it really him or his assertiveness that was affecting her?

Allowing herself to sink into the kiss, to lose herself in it, she waited…and waited for more.

But besides that momentary flutter, this kiss was the same as all the others they'd shared. A sweet, pleasant kiss. It didn't make her body hum with need or cause her toes to curl.

Damn it.

Don't be discouraged. There is something here. It might not be an over-the-top, runaway passion, but it will grow.

Allie had never had anything that was real before, nothing that would last. She just needed to be patient.

Allie pulled away and gave Hunter a reassuring smile. "We shouldn't do this here."

"Fine, I'll be a good boy, but what do you think about you and me grabbing a beer after work?"

"I would love to, but I have to get home and relieve Penny. She has to work at the Grizzly tonight."

Hunter stood up, running his hands from her waist down the sides of her thighs as he released her.

"Another time, then," he said, shooting her a wink before he unlocked her office door and slipped out.

Allie got home to find Dex up on the roof, hammering.

"Hey," she called.

He'd barely glanced up when she pulled in the driveway,

and his indifference was starting to grate on her. How could he say all of those things and then ignore her? He hadn't even thanked her for bringing him home when he was too drunk to do it himself.

Looking around for something to throw, she decided upon a pinecone. The goal was to toss it up onto the roof next to him to get his attention.

Instead, she'd hit him in the ass, and with more impact than she knew she had the ability to generate.

Dex jumped and looked at her over his shoulder with a glare. "What the hell?"

"Don't you have a job or something?"

"I told you I took some time off to fix all the things on the cabin. Is that why you tried to knock me off the roof?"

"Oh, please, it hardly touched you."

With a shake of his head, Dex turned back to his hammering. Heat crawled along Allie's skin, pricks of anger tightening her muscles as she worked herself into a full-on rage.

What an ass. He couldn't spare two seconds to acknowledge she'd done him a solid the other night?

Screw that.

Picking up another pinecone, this time she threw it with the full intention of hitting him on purpose.

Of course it whizzed over his head instead.

Figures.

"What the hell?" He spun around on his knees. "What's your problem?"

"You are, you selfish jerk!"

Before he could say anything to that, she stormed into the cabin and let out a shriek.

Penny glanced up from the textbook she was reading with Kermit sitting in her lap. "Rough day?"

Dex had no idea what had gotten into Allie, especially since she'd spent more than a week ignoring him. He couldn't really blame her. After the things he'd said to her and then that kiss...

He was actually surprised she hadn't slapped him outright.

He'd been drunk, admittedly, and he hadn't been able to stop railing on himself for being an inconsiderate dick, especially to Hunter. There was no reason for him to be so hung up on this one woman, so he'd made it his mission to do the right thing and stay away from her.

But now, the crazy lady was throwing things at him while he was on her freaking roof.

That shit would not stand.

An hour later, once Penny left, Dex climbed down the ladder and opened the door to the cabin without knocking.

Allie shut the fridge and turned on him, her brown eyes blazing. "I thought we agreed you would stop barging in here without knocking?"

"Actually, you said that. I chose to ignore you."

"Well, that's a big change."

"I want to know what your problem is."

"Oh, I don't know, Dex. Maybe it's the fact that I left my date early to drive your drunk ass home and I didn't even get a 'thank you.'"

"You want me to thank you, I'll th—"

"And, you not only spouted off a bunch of total bullshit that messed with my head, but then you kissed me."

Dex felt his face fall. "You're right. I was drinking, but that is no excuse to disrespect you while you were just trying to help me. I acted like an asshole. I'm sorry."

Allie seemed surprised by his admission, if her excessive blinking was any indication. "Thank you."

"You're welcome. So, are we good? Or are you going to continue to throw things at me like a twelve-year-old?"

Allie blushed. He secretly loved the way she looked when she was flushed, even if it wasn't for the reason he wanted her to be.

I just apologized for being a dick. I need to stop imagining Allie Fairchild flushed and moaning in the middle of my bed.

Chapter 15

ALLIE HAD NO idea what else to say now that Dex had apologized. Part of her screamed to show him the door, but that wasn't what she did.

"Are you hungry? I was going to pop a pizza in the oven, because I'm too tired and sore to really cook."

"Why are you so sore?"

"Just a lot going on at the hospital. Stress and I've been running around. No big."

Without saying anything, Dex walked to the freezer and pulled out the pizza. "How about you pour yourself a glass of wine and sit down. I'll put the pizza in the oven."

"No, really. That's okay. You've been doing so much on the cabin that I'm sure you're exhausted—"

Waving his hand at her, he laughed. "It's a frozen pizza, not a four-course meal. Seriously, go sit."

Allie wasn't going to stand there arguing, not when her lower back was crying out at her to sit down. Grabbing a bottle of wine and a glass, she sat on the couch. She poured a glass as Kermit trotted over and tried to jump up next to her. She picked the puppy up and let him crawl across her lap as she leaned back into the couch with a sigh.

She heard the tread of Dex's feet behind her before his hands even touched the sore muscles of her shoulders.

"What are you doing?" she asked.

"Making you feel good."

The way he said it, with an almost husky edge to his tone, sent a shiver down her spine. For the first time, she didn't fight him. She leaned back into his touch as he rubbed, thumbing the knots in her muscles firmly. It was heaven, and the irony that she'd received two massages from two completely different men in the same day did not escape her.

She was practically asleep by the time the oven beeped, alerting them that it was preheated, and he stopped his administrations. She turned around on the couch to watch him go back to the oven, teasing, "You know, if you ever get tired of the search-and-rescue gig, I think you'd kick ass as a masseur."

"Is that a fact?" He was bent over, his jeans-clad ass with its sexy leather tool belt facing her and spinning all kinds of dirty fantasies in her head. Should she ask him to take it off?

She shook her head to clear her thoughts.

Once the timer was set, Dex came back and her fantasy was realized. The tool belt came off and he set it down on the coffee table before sitting next to her on the couch. Spinning his finger in a circle, he said, "Turn around. I'll work out the kinks in your lower back."

Allie didn't even hesitate, just scooted around, pulling Kermit off her lap and setting him on the floor. She presented him her back and her skin hummed with anticipation as he spread the palms of his hands out and began to knead her sore muscles. His thumb and fingers worked at her, and she relaxed, moaning in utter ecstasy. She didn't even start when his hands crept up underneath her shirt, his rough, calloused hands against her smooth skin sending pleasure from her lower back down her thighs.

"God, that feels amazing." Allie hardly recognized her voice, it was so low.

Dex's hands lifted her shirt higher, and the cool air on her back broke through her stupor. She was just about to ask what he was doing when she felt something soft press against her spine.

His mouth. He was *kissing* her.

Another brush of his lips on her skin was electric, and she tensed. Not because she didn't like it, but because the sensation was wreaking havoc on her.

Dex's hands smoothed over her lower back and around her waist, splaying over her abdomen, and still, she didn't say no. Didn't want to say no.

He brought her back against him, his mouth finding the curve of her neck. With a sigh, she reached back, cupping his head with her hand. He twisted her around slowly until he had her draped across his lap, and when his lips closed over hers, it felt like she was being licked by a thousand flames.

Allie opened her lips to his tongue and moved her arms around his neck as he made love to her mouth. Hard and soft, light and teasing, and then his hand was tangled in her hair, pulling slightly until her scalp tingled. The drumming of desire between her thighs made her squeeze them together against the ache, wanting so much more than his kiss.

And then his hand was there, cupping the front of her pants, his finger sliding over her. She arched up into his touch as he rubbed her, and she could feel the warmth of his hands through her cotton panties.

He unfastened the clasp of her pants and slipped his hand inside, and when his finger found the nub of her clitoris, she jerked. He pressed harder, rubbing in tight, fast circles until she was gasping against his mouth, her nails digging into the back of his neck.

Oh, yes, I'm—

As her orgasm rocked her, sending tremors throughout her body, she saw bright, flashing lights behind her closed eyes. She came back down, slowly, and realized Dex was still brushing her lips softly, with gentle pecks that brought her back to reality.

Her eyes flew open, and met his bright green ones.

Good God, what did I just do?

Dex knew the moment was over when Allie opened her eyes. The horror in them was like a sucker punch.

Slipping his hand out of her pants, he refastened her slacks, taking his time without letting his gaze leave hers.

A few moments later, when the oven timer went off, Allie still hadn't moved or loosened her grip around his neck. Reaching up, he pulled her hands down and set them across her stomach with a pat. "I'll go get that."

After Allie scrambled off of him, he got up, silently cursing himself. How could he have let this happen? The moment he'd touched her, he knew he was doing something wrong. He should've left, gone home, taken a cold shower, and forgotten all about Allie—but he hadn't been able to stop. He'd waited for her to say no, to grab his hand, to do something...

But she hadn't. She'd melted into him, kissing him back so sweetly, and his mind had moved onto one track. Touching her, tasting her. Branding her as his.

It wasn't fair. It wasn't real. Whatever this attraction, this passion was between them, he wasn't the guy for her. He wasn't the long-haul, "get married and tuck the kids into bed every night" kind of man.

Hunter was, though. Hunter could give Allie what she wanted.

Dex went to the sink and washed his hands, gritting his teeth while the hard-on pressed painfully against the front of his jeans. Ignoring it as best he could, he slipped on Allie's oven mitts and pulled the pizza out. Once he'd set it on the counter, he cleared his throat.

"Look, I'm sorry. I let things get out of hand." With a dry

chuckle, he tried to go for nonchalant. "We can just forget this. Chalk it up to temporary insanity."

Allie stared blankly at him over the couch, her blond hair messy and her lips red and raw from his kisses. She was the most beautiful thing he'd ever seen, and yet, he was going to walk away. They needed some distance.

"Look, um…I'm gonna skip out on the pizza. But thanks for the invite. I'll just…I'll see you later."

Like a coward, he walked out the door without looking back. Because when he'd see the look of relief on her face, he wouldn't be able to handle it.

Chapter 16

HUNTER KNEW SOMETHING was going on with Allie. Over the last week she had been avoiding him and he couldn't figure out why. He'd invited her to dinner, left her flowers, and still, she kept coming up with excuses.

Suspicion clouded his mind, and armed with two coffees and a smile, he was determined to get to the bottom of it.

He tapped on her office door and poked his head in. "Hey, you got a second for coffee?"

And there it was, that guarded look. "Well, um…I have a lot of paperwork to finish."

Hunter's patience snapped and he closed the door behind him. "Allie, I feel like you're dodging me and I've got to know. Did I come on too strong or do something?"

"No, I mean…" Allie groaned, putting her face in her hands. When she finally looked up at him, her face was filled with regret. "I am so sorry I've made you feel like that…I've just…I've been confused and needed a little time."

"Confused about what?"

He waited for her to answer, holding his breath.

"Well...last week, Dex..." She took a deep breath, as if she were preparing herself for what she was about to say. "He kissed me...."

Blood pounded in Hunter's ears. "He kissed you."

"Yes, and I feel terrible about it—"

"Did you kiss him back?" Why was he even asking this? Of course she kissed him back; she wouldn't have avoided telling him about it if she hadn't.

"I...yes."

"I see." Taking a deep, shaky breath, he smiled. "It's okay. We weren't exclusive or anything. Are you interested in seeing him, or was this a onetime thing?"

"No, no, it just...happened. And he is definitely not interested in me. He told me that outright."

Hunter's fists clenched. *Asshole.*

It wasn't even the fact that Dex had kissed her—well, it was partly that he'd kissed her—but mostly, it was the lies that got to Hunter. Dex had told him he wasn't interested in Allie. Then he'd made a play for her and didn't say a word to Hunter about it? They'd had drinks several times over the past week and he'd had plenty of opportunity to bring it up.

And then, after kissing her, he'd told Allie he wasn't interested?

Hunter was about to lose his shit.

"I am so sorry." Her words were coming out a little choked.

Giving her a no-big-deal smile, he said, "It's okay. Really,

I…why don't we take a little break and you can take all the time you need to figure things out."

Allie's eyes were shiny with tears, but he was too keyed up right now to comfort her.

He needed a break himself, some air.

Hunter left Allie's office and headed downstairs and out the front door. Taking a few deep breaths, he closed his eyes and let the cold air seep into his lungs. A storm was coming, he could tell by the gray sky and the bite to the wind, and something about those gray clouds was calming. Helped clear his head.

Except then he heard Dex's voice. "Hey, man, what's up?"

Hunter's eyes flew open, and all of his fury, all of the betrayal and hurt that had been churning inside him, boiled up and over as he launched himself at Dex.

Chapter 17

AFTER DEX HAD finished the roof on the cabin, he'd gone into town for a case of beer and some essentials. After two weeks, the cabin looked better than it had in twenty years.

And he guessed he had Allie to thank.

He had to admit, he'd wimped out, the way he'd up and left like that, but Allie hadn't exactly reached out to him, either. Clearly, she didn't want to discuss what had happened.

But he was still her landlord, and now that he'd finished his work, he needed to reevaluate the rental agreement with her. He'd figured the safest place to talk was the hospital, where they wouldn't be completely alone and he wouldn't be tempted to kiss her again.

But when he'd approached the entrance, he'd seen Hunter standing out front by the big oak, looking a little nauseated.

Dex had called out a greeting as he approached, but when Hunter opened his eyes, Dex had paused and took in his molten red face and furious expression.

She'd told him.

"Ah, hell—oomph!"

Hunter tackled him to the ground, and for the second time in two weeks, Dex had the wind knocked out of him.

"You son of a bitch!" Hunter threw a right hook that made Dex's cheek explode. The same cheek the biker had punched, too. Stars popped around Hunter's head as Dex tried to focus. "Lying piece of shit, you're supposed to be my best friend."

Dex recovered his wits enough to raise his arms to protect his face, and as soon as Hunter's weight shifted, he bucked, dislodging Hunter. He climbed to his feet and held out his hands in defense.

"It's not what you think, Hunt—"

"What I think is that I told you I was interested in Allie, and you said go for it. Then, the minute my back was turned, you made a play for her. That's what I think."

Dex couldn't argue the semantics, but it was more complicated than that. "I didn't mean to kiss her, it just—"

"Don't say it just happened. That's a cop-out and you know it. Man up and tell me you want her. Don't be a coward."

"I don't want her, okay?" Dex yelled. "I don't. I am not interested in her, not for anything more than a casual f—"

Dex closed his mouth when he saw her, standing in the crowd he hadn't even noticed. This time, he couldn't walk away from the pain on her face. It became ingrained in his memory.

Hunter grabbed him up by his shirt, and he waited for the blow he deserved. It never came.

Hunter shoved him away from him, disgust oozing from his tone. "You're not worth it."

As Hunter turned and walked away toward the side entrance, Dex glanced back to where Allie had been standing, but she was gone.

Allie wiped at her red, wet eyes as she searched for Hunter, trying to avoid every gaze that followed her as she passed. It had only been ten minutes, but she knew people were gossiping, speculating about her and what she'd done to cause two grown men to fight over her in front of *her* hospital.

Seems like she'd figured out a new way to screw up her life. She had been in town for barely three weeks and she'd managed not only to pit two best friends against each other but to discredit herself in front of her staff.

She'd tried to fight the tears, but what Dex had been about to say hurt. She'd known, deep down, that she didn't mean anything to him. That what happened had been a mistake, but having him announce it in front of everyone…

It had been hard to hide the effect that'd had on her.

Allie opened the door to one of the on-call rooms and found Hunter lying back on one of the bunks.

He glanced her way as she came inside and locked the door. "What are you doing?"

Allie held up the first aid kit she was carrying. "I thought you could use some patching up."

"I'm fine."

Allie ignored him and sat down on the bunk next to him. Opening up the kit, she pulled out an alcohol pad and ripped it open. She picked up his right knuckle, cracked and bruised, and gently wiped at the blood crusting. When he hissed in pain, she blew on it softly until he relaxed.

"You don't have to do this."

She smoothed the antiseptic ointment over his knuckle and wrapped a layer of gauze around it. "I want to." Once it was secured with tape, she set it back down along his side. "I'm really sorry. I never wanted to cause problems between the two of you."

"The problem is that he lied to me. It has nothing to do with you." He turned to look at her, piercing her with those blue eyes. "Can I ask you something?"

"Of course."

"Do you…do you have feelings for me? Or was that all in my head?"

"Yes, I do, it's just—"

"You have feelings for him, too? Be honest."

Allie didn't want to answer, but he deserved the truth. "I don't know exactly what I feel for him. Right now, I'm disgusted with him and myself, but—"

"Look, I'm not giving you some ultimatum. I'm not that guy, and despite how things are between us right now, Dex is a friend of mine. I'm not taking myself out of the running, but you don't owe me anything, either."

Then, to her surprise, he leaned up and cupped the back of

her head, bringing her down for a hard, fast kiss that caused another stir inside her. When he released her, she was a little dazed by it.

"What was that?" she whispered.

"That? That was something to think about."

Chapter 18

DEX WAS SITTING on the front porch of the cabin when Allie got home from work. When Allie saw him, her hands tightened on the steering wheel before she turned the car off and stepped out. Her stomach twisted and churned, tying her insides up in knots as she approached.

Dex stood up. "Allie—"

"Don't. Just don't."

His full lips compressed into a hard line, and she could tell his green eyes were blazing in the porch light.

"Fine, I just came by to apologize for earlier. What I said was out of line, and I'm sorry."

"Okay." Allie wished her voice hadn't trembled on the word as she tried to pass him. When he reached out to try to stop her, she said, "Don't you dare touch me."

Dex threw his hands up in the air. "All right, I won't, but we still need to talk."

"About what?"

"About the cabin. I finished the repairs and we need to talk about rent."

Allie gaped at him, completely taken aback. After everything that had happened, he was here for money? She stiffened and said, "Don't worry, Mr. Belmont, I'll have the check to you first thing tomorrow morning."

"Come on, Allie—"

"Good night."

With a heavy sigh, he let her pass, and she pushed through the door, slamming it behind her.

Penny held up a bottle of wine. "So I heard you had an interesting afternoon."

"How did you hear that?"

"My phone's been blowing up all day with questions about you. All the single men in town want to do you, and the women want to know what your secret is. I mean, if you can get two guys like Dex Belmont and Hunter Gracin to have a parking-lot brawl, you've gotta be dynamite in the sack."

"Kill me now," Allie groaned.

"No way! You are stirring things up around here. I mean, the most drama this town sees is on *The Bachelor*. You, my friend, are my new hero."

Allie grabbed two wineglasses from the cupboard and held one out to Penny. "Don't you have a bar to work at?"

"Called in sick. Figured you could use a little more estrogen and a lot less testosterone in your life."

"What I need is a time machine."

"Sorry, all out of TARDISes," Penny said as she poured Allie a glass of wine, nearly full to the brim. "But a few of these might help you block it all out for a little while."

The next morning, Dex slammed his fists into the sides of his punching bag, putting all of his self-loathing and bitterness into every blow. God, he had messed everything up, even his apology. He hadn't meant to talk about rent at all, but when she'd tried to blow past him without giving him a chance to explain, he'd lashed out.

Bluebell let out a loud howl as someone pounded on his front door.

Dex, shirtless and covered in sweat, jogged from his gym room to answer it and found Allie standing on his front step with an envelope.

"Here you go. You are paid up for six months, so there is no reason for us to have any other contact except in a professional capacity."

Dex took the envelope, slapping it against his thigh. "Come on, Allie, I get that I handled all of this badly, but we live next door to each other. We are going to see each other around town."

"Seeing each other out and about is fine. It's the being-alone-together part we have a problem with."

Hoping to break through her anger, he tried to tease her. "Are you saying that you have no self-control when it comes to me?"

Her dark-brown eyes were so cold, his smile slipped. "Actually, at this moment, I wouldn't touch you if you were the last man on earth."

With that, Allie spun on her heels and walked to her Jetta. Dex watched her disappear down the road, and when she was out of sight, he slammed the door. Bluebell was lying across the floor watching him pace, and for some reason, he found himself talking to the dog.

"Why can't she just accept that I messed up? We all make mistakes and say things we shouldn't. It's not as if I set out to hurt her."

Bluebell lifted her head and yawned, but Dex kept talking.

"I mean, I said I was sorry, and she's not exactly innocent. She kissed me back; she let me...."

God, when she'd come on his hand, all he'd wanted to do was rip off her pants and bury himself inside her. To make love to her until she was screaming *his* name. He'd wanted to possess her, to brand her as his. It had scared the hell out of him.

So he'd taken the easy way out and bailed. He'd pushed her away and that made him a horrible guy.

And even more, he was the guy who lost his best friend.

Sitting on the couch, he rubbed his hands over his face, breathing deep. When Bluebell stuck her wet nose under his chin and nuzzled him, he let his hands drop to stroke her soft ears.

"I guess I really screwed up this time, huh, girl?"

Chapter 19

THE FIRST MAJOR snowstorm of the season raged around Allie as she stood over her car engine, cursing. It was just past nine in the evening, freezing, and Allie wished for the millionth time that she'd left work before the storm hit, but with half her staff gone for Thanksgiving, she'd stayed late to help.

I could be back in New York right now.

But even surviving a blizzard was better than taking snide comments from her mother and long-winded lectures from her father for four days. No. Allie had decided to weather the storm from the warmth of her cabin. Instead, her car wouldn't start and the cold was eating through her clothes, numbing her skin painfully.

Out of the darkness and swirling snow, a buzzing engine and single headlight zoomed into the parking lot. The snow-mobile stopped behind her car, and the bundled-up driver got up, making his way toward her.

She recognized his strut before he even took off his helmet. *Dex.* She'd actually managed to avoid him for the past two weeks, even the few times she'd gone out with Penny or Hunter and a few other people from the hospital. She hadn't asked Hunter if the two of them were talking, because she didn't think it was her place.

"Are you all right?" Dex asked loudly. His deep baritone swirled around her in the wind, and she shivered, a reflex she swore was from the cold and not because she'd missed the sound of his voice.

"I'm fine." This was the first conversation they'd had in weeks, and she still wasn't ready for it.

"Sure you are. That's why you're standing outside, staring under your hood in a blizzard, right?"

He had a point. "My car won't start."

Dex ducked inside, flipping on a flashlight she hadn't seen in his other hand. "Your battery is probably frozen. Have you checked it lately?"

"No, I've been busy."

"Well, NAPA is closed by now. Here"—he handed her his helmet—"hop on the back and I'll give you a ride home."

She shoved the helmet back at him, a little harder than necessary. "Thanks, but I'll get a ride from someone in-side."

Even in the dark storm, the parking-lot light showed that his green eyes were blazing. "Are you seriously going to make someone drive out of their way in a snowstorm just to spite me?"

"I'll stay with Penny, then."

With a shake of his head that sent snow flying off his hair, he said, "Suit yourself."

But as he walked back to his snowmobile, Allie reconsidered her options. Penny had left Allie's place before the storm hit, meaning Kermit had been locked in his cage for at least four hours. There was no way in hell she was going to ask Dex to check in on him. She didn't need to owe him any more favors.

Thinking about Kermit's adorable, lonely face as he lay locked in his cage, though…

"Wait!" Slamming the hood of her car down and grabbing her purse off the front seat, she trudged through the snow to catch up.

He paused, straddling the snowmobile and watching her with one raised eyebrow.

"Can you please give me a ride home?"

Folding his arms, the helmet still dangling from his hand, he seemed to be considering. Unlike her shivering body, he appeared oblivious to the cold, and it made her hate him more than she already did.

If I really hated him, then I wouldn't think about him a hundred times a day.

"Say 'I'm sorry, Dex, for being rude' first," he said.

"What are you, five?" she asked.

He didn't respond, just sat there with that annoying eyebrow arched, waiting expectantly.

She decided she could still despise someone and be attracted to them. Through gritted teeth, she muttered, "I'm sorry, Dex, for being rude."

Giving her the helmet, he waited until she was on the back of the snowmobile with her arms wrapped around him before he started the engine. As he blazed out of the parking lot and up the road toward home, she held on tight, the wind in her face like a thousand needles piercing her skin. Finally, she laid her cheek against Dex's back and closed her eyes. The ride was bumpy and long, and by the time he pulled into his garage, she was shaking so badly she could hardly stand.

"Why don't you come inside and get warmed up?" he asked.

"No, thanks, I've got to let Kermit out."

"I can get Kermit—"

"It's not going to happen," she said harshly. Taking a deep breath, she tried again with a little less bite to it. "Thank you very much for the ride. Good night."

She turned and made her way out of the warm garage and up the hill toward the cabin, the snow blinding her. Finally, she burst inside and flipped on the light so she could see Kermit, but nothing happened. She continued fiddling with the switch, and finally groaned in frustration. She could hear Kermit whimpering and realized how frigid it was *inside*.

As if the heat had been off for hours.

The dark and the cold were beginning to cause a claustrophobic tightness to wrap around her. She had always hated the dark, because her imagination always went to what might be lurking there. Fumbling in her purse for her phone, she called Dex, trying to make her way toward Kermit's cage by feel.

"Change your mind about coming over?"

"No, but my power is out and I can't see anything. Can you bring a flashlight and flip the breakers for me?"

She could hear his heavy sigh through the phone. "Why don't you bring Kermit and wait out the storm with me? I have a backup generator and a fireplace—"

"God, can't you just, for once, do something nice without acting like it is an inconvenience to you?" Her voice came out shrill and panicked. Silence on the other end had her checking to see if the call had dropped, but no, he was still there.

Way to go. Insult the only person who can help.

"I didn't mean that, I just…I don't like the dark."

After what seemed like forever, he finally spoke. "I'll be right there."

As Dex came through the door, the snow slid down his neck and under his collar, making him shiver. Or maybe it was the freezing, dark room. No wonder Allie hadn't wanted to go searching for the breaker box.

Turning on the flashlight, he shone it around the room until he found her sitting on the couch, holding Kermit.

"Are you okay?"

"Yeah. I couldn't find my flashlight or I would have gone out and tried to flip them myself," she said.

"Well, come stand at the door and let me know if anything

happens when I try the breakers. The less time I stay out in the cold, the better."

Allie stood up and he could hear the tread of her feet behind him as she followed him to the door. He went around the side of the cabin and yanked the box open. He started pushing the breakers back and forth. "Anything?"

"No, nothing."

"Shit." Closing the box, he hurried back into the house, as if it would be any warmer there than outside.

"You can't fix it?"

"No, not in this weather. You're going to have to stay at my place tonight, so why don't you go grab a few things—"

"Honestly, I'll be fine. I'll build a fire and add some extra blankets to my bed."

He tried to hang on to his temper, but she was being so pigheaded it wasn't easy. "Damnit, woman! It's only going to get colder out there, which means the temperature is going to drop considerably in here as the night goes on. So, why don't you stop being stubborn and make this easy on all of us, including Kermit. You don't want him to freeze just because you don't like me, do you?"

He could tell she was fighting the urge to tell him to go to hell, just from the expression on her face.

"I appreciate your concern, but I'll let him snuggle with me. We'll be good."

Running a hand over his face, he made the decision that was going to piss her off the most.

Taking Kermit from her, he ignored her protests. "If you want to freeze to death, fine, but he's coming with me."

He marched toward the door as she hurled curses at his back.

"You're a jackass, you know that?"

Pausing at the door, he tossed her an exasperated look over his shoulder. "I'm not the one sitting in a dark, cold room because she doesn't want to accept help. I hope you and your wounded pride are happy together."

He stormed out of the cabin, waiting for a moment to see if she would follow, but she didn't.

To hell with her, then. He'd tried to be a good guy, and she'd thrown it back in his face.

He was done.

Chapter 20

SEVERAL HOURS LATER, Allie lay huddled in her bed, shivering under four blankets. Her hooded sweatshirt was pulled up over her head and she'd lost all feeling in her nose. She'd nearly gotten out of bed several times and crossed the hundred yards to bang on Dex's door, but had been worried he wouldn't answer. Then she'd have been even more humiliated and cold than she already was.

Besides, he'd been a jerk, anyway, throwing that line about "wounded pride" at her. Just because she didn't want to accept his help more than she needed to didn't mean she was too proud.

At this point, though, she wasn't feeling terribly concerned with owing him anything. Especially since she couldn't seem to get her toes warm.

A noise coming from the kitchen brought her head up, and her stomach tightened in fear. Had the raccoons found a way back in?

Her bedroom door opened and the dark form in her doorway shone a flashlight in her face, blinding her.

"Ah, what the hell?" she cried.

"You are the biggest pain in the ass I have ever met, you know that?" Dex's deep voice growled. He came around the side of the bed, and without waiting for her to say anything, he picked her up, swaddled in the blankets, and headed for the door.

"You don't have to carry me. I give in. You were right."

"I'm not taking any chances that you'll change your mind. I almost left you here all night to teach you a lesson."

"Why didn't you?"

She silently begged him to say something. If Dex had been worried about her, it meant he had to care for her, even if only a little bit.

Right?

"Because I'm a bigger idiot than you."

Well, that wasn't terribly flattering.

"Get the door for me, will you?" he asked.

She reached down to turn the knob and, once they were through, pulled it behind them. His porch light was like a beacon in the storm and she snuggled her face into the front of his jacket, trying to warm her nose.

"Are you nuzzling me?"

"No, my nose is cold. I'm trying to rub the feeling back."

"Well, try not to get snot on my jacket."

Allie stopped and sniffed. She couldn't tell if her nose was running or not, but why take the chance?

On second thought, after what a jerk he'd been, a little snot was the least he deserved.

Finally, when they were both inside his house, the warm air hit her face and she sighed in pure bliss as her numb skin started to tingle.

"I'm going to set you on the couch and get you something warm to drink. Do you want coffee or whisky?"

"I better stick with the coffee," she said. "Whisky and I don't make the best of friends."

Dex grinned as he gazed down at her, the familiarity in his gaze making her heart ache. "I happen to remember you and whisky rather fondly."

No, she couldn't do this. She couldn't let his teasing or his sexy smile break down her resolve. She couldn't get hurt again.

The thought startled her. The last few weeks she'd been angry, with herself and with Dex, but she hadn't really thought about the fact that she had been hurt by him, too. Because despite some of his less-than-stellar moments, she'd actually started to like Dex. He made her laugh, even when she didn't want to, and he had moments of caring that showed a sweet side of him.

Of course, he didn't have a single characteristic on her list. Okay, maybe one or two, but the point was that no matter what she'd started to feel for Dex, he'd squashed it. She was over it, and the first thing she could do to prove that was to let go of her anger.

With a bit of a sad smile, she said, "After everything that's happened, I think we better not dwell too much on that."

He was silent, making his way around the kitchen. She could hear Kermit whining from somewhere. "Hey, where's my dog?"

"Locked in his old crate with a blanket. He's warm at least, which is more than I can say for you."

Considering how her skin stung as the feeling came back into her fingers and face, she hoped so.

"Why do you always have your dog locked up when I come over?"

"Because sometimes you stop by during her dinnertime."

"Your dog has a set dinnertime?" she asked.

"No, I just usually lock her up with a bone while I have dinner, and then I let her out when we go to bed."

Allie turned to see him in the kitchen, her eyebrows raised. "We?"

"Yes, *we*. You are not the only one who loves your dog. Bluebell usually takes the left side of the bed and shoves me all the way to the right by the time the alarm clock goes off."

Allie laughed at the image of the big bloodhound kicking her master out of bed. Dex gave her a boyish smile in return. The one that set off a hundred fluttering wings in her abdomen.

"Do you want milk and sugar?" he asked.

She told herself to stop thinking about him in that way.

Maybe they could move past everything and be friends. "Yes, please, both."

He brought her over a steaming mug. "Scoot closer to the fire if you need to."

"Thanks." She took the mug, the ceramic scalding her skin. Setting it down on the side table to cool, she stared into the burning fire, more than aware when Dex sat next to her. Allie watched him drink his coffee out of the corner of her eye, his full lips on the brim, the sexy Adam's apple bobbing in his throat when he swallowed. She worked up the nerve to say something...well, nice.

"Thank you for coming back for me. I know I didn't give you a reason to with the way I behaved."

"It's fine. I'm sorry for what I said." He drummed his fingers on the mug and then added, "Besides, I couldn't let you suffer out there. It would have gone against my code."

Fighting the blankets surrounding her, she tucked her feet up on the couch and turned to face him. "You have a code? I never would have thought."

"Why?" he asked. "Because I made out with my best friend's girl?"

The words instantaneously killed the ease she was just starting to feel with him.

"I didn't mean it like that."

"I know, but I did. I should never have touched you."

"I wasn't Hunter's girl, though." He stiffened next to her and her cheeks finally warmed as she realized how that had sounded. "I just mean…we had only been out a few times and we weren't exclusive."

He actually turned on the couch to face her, pulling her gaze to his with those intense green eyes. "And now?"

"We're just friends." Clearing her throat, she asked, "Why are you asking? It's not like you're interested. You said I was just casual, right?"

"About that—" he started to say, but she couldn't bear to hear his excuses.

"No, you don't need to apologize again. Not after all this time. I get it. You're one of those guys who has to tap every woman he comes in contact with."

"Not *every* woman. In fact, I haven't tapped anyone, as you say, since you showed up."

Allie's gut clenched. "What the hell are you doing?"

"Being honest?" he said.

How dare he?

Flinging off the blankets, she stood up angrily. "Whatever game you're playing with me, it's not funny or fair. I appreciate you letting me stay here and helping me out tonight, but you were more than clear about what your endgame was with me. And I'm not interested in that. Backpedaling or acting like there's something more going on here because you're horny isn't going to work."

"Hear me out, because I swear I'm not backpedaling right now." He grabbed her hand and looked her square in the eye. "I never would have said what I did if I'd known you were there. Hunter had caught me off guard and I was just running my mouth to get him off my back about lying to him. Besides, you weren't."

"I wasn't what?" she asked.

"Casual. I didn't kiss you because you were just there. I did it because I wanted to." His voice lowered. "I wanted you. I still do."

Her heart thumped loudly in her chest. What the hell did she say to that? While the part of her that was still hurt and angry wanted to get up and walk away, she couldn't deny that the words *I still want you, too* sat poised on the tip of her tongue.

But he'd had a chance to step in and be with her, and he'd blown it.

"I can't." She headed for the hallway, abandoning her coffee and her desires in his living room as she escaped.

"Allie?" he called.

She paused, waiting for him to ask her not to go. To stay up, talk to him, and figure this whole mess out.

"Second door on the left."

Dex sat on his couch, shooting back another whisky as he stared into the fire.

What the hell had he expected her to say? That she wanted him, too, despite everything? And when had he decided to go all true confessions on her, anyway?

Truth was, he'd caught himself making his way to her place

several times over the last few weeks. He wasn't sure what he would have said when he got there, because he never made it to her door. One thing was for sure, though: Allie Fairchild hadn't been far from his thoughts.

Which should have been enough to make him stay the hell away from her, except…he didn't want to. For the first time, he didn't think of being with a woman as something to avoid. Allie made him want to be better than a jerk who seduced a girl behind his best friend's back. She was different.

But how the hell could he convey all that to *her* when he could barely process what it all meant to him? He knew that he wanted her and had feelings for her, but what did that mean? And was it enough to make him keep trying to earn her forgiveness, or would it just end up leaving them both disappointed?

And it didn't just involve him and Allie. Hunter had just started to forgive him, and despite Allie's assurance that she wasn't Hunter's girl, how would Hunter feel if Dex admitted he had real feelings for Allie? That she actually got him thinking about all the things that used to send him running?

Dex set his glass down with a groan, massaging his aching forehead with his fingers. God, why was this shit so complicated?

Chapter 21

ALLIE WOKE UP the next morning disoriented and exhausted. She'd tossed and turned half the night before finally drifting off after she'd heard Dex's steps outside her door. For the briefest moment, she'd imagined him opening it and stepping inside. He'd tell her again how sorry he was and offer to do anything to make it up to her.

The fantasy had been enough to put her to sleep, but it still felt like there was a sledgehammer currently beating inside her head. Getting out of the bed, she tried to straighten the covers and then tiptoed into the hallway. She was hoping Dex was still asleep, so she could grab Kermit and sneak out.

Except she didn't have any shoes. Crap. Maybe she could slip on a pair of his tennis shoes.

One glance out the big bay windows made her heart sink. She wasn't sneaking out, at least not in tennis shoes. Outside was completely white, with several feet of snow covering the ground and still more coming down in a dense whiteout.

"Good morning," Dex called from the kitchen, startling her.

"Hi. Any idea when this is supposed to let up?" Allie tried to look anywhere but Dex's bare chest, but was losing the battle. It was just so defined and chiseled.

"My weather app says it's going to continue through tomorrow night. I hope you don't have to work."

"No, but if there is a break in the weather, I'll have to get my phone in case there is an emergency at the hospital."

His deep chuckle rose gooseflesh over her skin as he approached in just a pair of sweats and his bare feet. "Not sure what kind of break you're expecting. It's only going to get worse from here. The only good thing to come out of heavy snow like this is the winter tourists who show up to snowboard, ski, and snowmobile."

Allie loved to snowboard when she was a teenager, but she hadn't been in years. With Bear Mountain Ski Resort just up the road, she supposed she'd get a chance to pick it up again. "I guess that means things pick up for you again, huh? Having to rescue people from snowdrifts or avalanches?"

"Not very often. I was actually hoping for a little peace and quiet."

"Don't you need to make a living?" she asked.

"Well, between acts of heroism, I work for the National Park Service as a ranger. I patrol the area, make sure people aren't being stupid and trespassing."

"A jack-of-all-trades," she said. "Why search-and-rescue?"

"Because I enjoy it. Most people who get lost are found cold or hungry, but relatively unharmed. But when they see me coming, they are damn happy I'm there. I can say I do it for the adrenaline rush, but that's only part of it. I want to help people, to feel needed. Useful. I do it for that look on their face that says I'm the guy they've been waiting for."

Allie paused and stared into Dex's eyes. She understood that. Allie had become a nurse to help people, and an administrator to make a difference. And even though her job function required that she make things better for the hospital system as a whole, she did it because she was helping individuals get the care they needed.

Suddenly, she and Dex were looking a hell of a lot more similar.

Dex made coffee, wishing that he could read Allie's mind. He couldn't imagine she was happy to be stuck with him for at least a day, but she seemed content enough. She'd just curled up on the couch with Kermit, staring quietly at the falling snow outside.

"The coffee should be ready in a minute. How would you feel about some breakfast?" he asked.

"Sure, that would be great. Thanks."

He went about the kitchen, pulling out eggs, potatoes, peppers, onions, and cheese. "Do omelets and country potatoes sound good?"

"Like heaven." She was snuggling Kermit, Bluebell dogging her steps as she walked into the kitchen. "Will she hurt him if I put him down?"

"She might lick him to death, but that's about the extent of her viciousness," he said.

As Allie set Kermit on the ground, Dex was pretty sure she called him an ass under her breath, but he let it go. Maybe it was because she was actually talking to him, or that he had her all to himself for another twenty-four hours, but he started whistling joyfully.

"Do you have family?" she asked.

He stopped whistling. "Sure. My parents and my little brother live in Philadelphia."

"Why didn't you go home to visit them for Thanksgiving?"

Beating the eggs with his whisk, he shrugged. "We're not exactly the warm-and-fuzzy type. I love my family, but I'm a bit of an odd duck to them."

"How's that?"

"Mainly because I preferred camping and fishing to studying."

"Ah," she said. "My parents don't understand me, either. Thought I would have been better off marrying a man with an education than getting one."

"That's too bad." Dex started cutting up the ingredients. "I like that you're smart."

Allie cleared her throat. "Can I help?"

"Sure, just wash your hands and—"

"Yes. Jeez, I was a nurse. I wouldn't touch the food with dog cooties all over me."

Dex grinned. "My apologies, Nurse Fairchild."

"Like I was saying, I didn't want to spend the rest of my

life married to a politician or CEO, organizing teas and charity auctions. It took me a while to find my calling, but when I did, nothing was going to stand in my way."

Dex had to admit he was surprised by her admission. Allie might be a stubborn, infuriating woman, but she didn't exactly scream rebel.

"I take it you didn't go home because you didn't want to deal with their judgment?" he asked.

"Exactly." She smiled at him over the green bell pepper she was cutting, and he opened his mouth to warn her right before the knife came down. She cried out and cradled her hand, and he was at her side in a second.

"Let me see." She allowed him to examine the side of her thumb, which had been neatly sliced on its side. He grabbed a clean hand towel from the cupboard and wrapped it tightly to stanch the blood. He noticed her wince and mumbled an apology.

"I have a first aid kit in the bathroom. Come on. You sit on the couch and wait while I grab it."

He held the towel around her finger as he led her toward the couch, leaving her there to retrieve the first aid kit. When he got back, her face was sheet-white.

As he kneeled down, he teased lightly, "You're not going to faint on me, are you? Might have to kiss you if you pass out on my couch. Maybe even cop a feel."

"Pervert." A ghost of a smile played across her lips, even as pain filled her eyes, wet with unshed tears.

He pulled back the towel and the cut started bleeding again. Dex was half tempted to put her on the snowmobile and take her up for some stitches, but it was nasty out there and hardly worth endangering their lives for a stitch or two when he could do them just as well.

"Think you can man up while I clean, stitch, and wrap this? It will hurt like a mother, but I think I have some Tylenol with codeine or might even have a couple of Valium."

"Tylenol is fine. Narcotics make me sick." Weakly, she slapped his shoulder. "That's for stringing together one very sexist sentence."

"What? Woman up, then. For a nurse, you're pretty squeamish. It's cute."

"I can handle other people's blood, but I get woozy when I see my own," she said.

He handed her the pain pill and finished doctoring her thumb. He patted her knee comfortingly. "I'll get you some water."

She covered his hand with hers, and held it to her knee. His gaze rose to meet hers, and he was shocked when she leaned over and kissed him. It wasn't anything more than a peck, but it left him wanting to bury his hands in her hair and bring her back for more.

Instead, he just smiled as he stood up. "You're welcome."

Chapter 22

"YOU'RE A CHEATER!" Dex's green eyes danced as he said it, so she didn't take it personally. It was nearly seven in the evening, and since the snow was still going strong, they had spent the day watching movies and playing card games. Dex had been the one to suggest a game of slapjack, and she couldn't help if she was better at it than he was.

"Am not! I'm just faster."

"You totally pushed my hand out of the way," he said.

"Wow, I didn't know such a big man could be such a sore loser."

"You know what? You're gonna pay."

Allie squealed and jumped up from the table, laughing as she ran. Bluebell and Kermit chased after her, yipping and howling, but she didn't get very far. Dex's arms wrapped around her from behind and he lifted her up, spinning them in a circle until she was dizzy.

"Uncle! Uncle!"

He stopped and turned her to face him, practically wheezing with laughter.

"Do you confess to your dirty, rotten cheating ways?"

"Never!"

God, when was the last time I've laughed this hard?

"Then I have no choice but to tickle you into submission." His fingers attacked her ribs and she screamed, reaching to grab his hands…

And then cried out when her injured finger got bumped.

He stopped wrestling her and gently took her hand in his. "Are you okay?"

"Yeah, I just forgot for a minute," she said, her voice tight with pain. The first pill had made her drowsy, so she'd been holding off from taking another.

"Me, too. I'm sorry."

To her surprise, he raised her hand up and placed a gentle kiss on the palm.

She caught her breath as the spot warmed with the press of his lips and breath. Allie stared at him, their eyes locked, and the air around them practically sizzled.

"Allie?"

"Yeah?"

"Am I going to have to apologize again?" he asked.

"For what?"

He trailed his fingers over her cheek gently, taking a step closer. "If I kiss you right now, am I going to have to apologize later?"

Her heart skipped as understanding sank in. This was it. Did she take another leap and give him one more chance? Or did she pull away?

Dex dropped his hand and started to move back, obviously taking her hesitation as a refusal. With her good hand, she grabbed the front of his shirt, stopping him in his tracks.

"Only if you stop."

The shift in Dex's expression stole her breath away and in the next moment, his lips claimed hers. Mindful of her sore thumb, she hooked her other arm around the back of his neck, giving in to his kiss and the touch of his hands, which seemed to be everywhere at once. Her arms, her shoulders, her neck…it was as if he couldn't stop tracing every curve of her body. With a sigh, she melted into him. This was what she'd been craving, not the quick, fiery passions of her past, or the tepid stirrings of Hunter's kisses.

Dex was like a warm wave, rolling in and picking her up, carrying her through pure bliss. Briefly she wondered if her issues with Dex had to do with them both fighting what they wanted. If they had just given in and let things develop the way they were meant to, would they have gotten here sooner?

She couldn't deny that she felt it. In his kiss, and the way his arms held her against him, it was as if he couldn't get enough of her. And never wanted to let her go.

They stumbled toward the bedroom, their clothes leaving a trail down the hallway. The last thing he wanted her to do was change her mind, especially as every brush of her bare skin against his felt like an electric shock.

In the most fantastic way.

No one else existed in this room but the two of them. He'd shut out Bluebell and Kermit, ignoring their protests, too caught up in the way Allie slid her bra down her arms, her full breasts falling beautiful and free.

And all mine.

The possessive thought didn't even stall him as he tossed his last bit of clothing, his boxer briefs, across the room, and pulled her to him. His mouth found the pulse at her neck, and moved down over her shoulder and across her collarbone, worshipping her body. Dex wanted to explore every inch of her until she came apart in his arms while he was buried inside her, rocking them both into oblivion.

The tips of her fingers slid into his hair, bringing his gaze up to hers. The look on her face was gentle. Smiling. Soft.

Love.

And that's when Dex realized why he'd never been the type to commit, why he'd fought so hard against settling down.

He'd been waiting for Allie.

She was stubborn and obstinate and a giant pain in the ass…but she was also funny, caring, and her beauty was so arresting that sometimes he had a hard time looking away from her.

As he kneeled before her, his lips made their way down her torso. He lost himself in the symphony of her pleasure, working his mouth over her sensitive flesh until she shattered against him.

Lifting her onto the bed and laying her down across his comforter, he took it all in. He'd spent the last five weeks imagining what she'd look like sprawled across his bed with her arms open for him.

Now he didn't have to fantasize anymore.

Once he had the condom on, he crawled up and over her, claiming her mouth once more as he flexed his hips. Her legs wrapped around him and he slid home, groaning in ecstasy as her warmth engulfed him. Rocking against her, he got lost in the taste and feel of her, the sweet sounds of her little moans as he buried his head in her neck, relishing the squeeze of her muscles around his cock as she came again.

When he followed her down, he knew. It had never been this good, felt this right.

It was all Allie.

And this time, he wasn't going to mess it up.

Chapter 23

ON SUNDAY MORNING, Dex waited in the parking lot of the hospital for Hunter. It was hard to stop smiling, considering how he'd spent the last three days with Allie. Besides making love, they had talked…about their childhoods and their friends. His time in the army and her failed attempt to appear on some reality singing competition when she was eighteen. Who knew being snowed in could be the most fun he'd had in…well, his whole life.

It was the second day since the snow had stopped and he needed to be back at work, especially since the avalanche danger level was high. He'd snuck out from under Allie's soft body, resisted her sleepy attempts to lure him back to bed, and stopped off in town for two coffees. One would be a peace offering for Hunter. Dex was hoping he'd get to keep his friend, but he wasn't counting his chickens yet.

Hunter pulled up next to him, and when he climbed out of his car, he gave Dex a nod.

"What's this?" Hunter asked.

"Coffee, with a side of 'We need to talk.'"

Hunter came around the front and took the proffered cup. "Aw, are you breaking up with me?"

The joke didn't have the same tone to it, not after the last five weeks. There was a definite edge to it, and Dex wasn't going to bullshit his friend. Not anymore.

"Look, I know that I've screwed up, especially with things between us, but I gotta be honest—"

"You slept with Allie."

Hunter didn't sound ready to throw the scalding coffee in his face, so he took that as a good sign.

"It's not like that. I…" *Ah, hell, spit it out.* "I care about her, Hunt. I didn't know it, or at the very least, wasn't ready to admit it, but I do. A lot."

Hunter took a drink from the coffee cup before saying, "Well, that's it, then."

"If you want to take a swing at me…wait, what does that mean?"

"It means I knew after you kissed her I had lost. I just figured you'd lost, too, when you acted like a total prick. But she gave you another chance?"

"Not at first. Her battery died and her power was out, so she stayed at my place—"

"I don't need details, really. Good for you, though. It seems like she makes you happy."

"She does, I'm not gonna lie. I'm really lucky." Dex was at a loss. Of all the ways he'd expected Hunter to react, cool and collected hadn't been among them. "Well, thanks, man. I appreciate it."

"I'm not going to do cartwheels, at least not anytime soon, but I also am not going to hold a grudge against you for falling for someone." Then Hunter grinned as he added, "Besides, with you off the market, the next hot, single woman that rolls into town will be all mine. No contest."

Holding his coffee cup out to his friend, he gave a toast. "Here's to love."

Hunter's eyebrows shot up his forehead. "Love, huh?"

Dex shrugged with a sheepish smile. "What can I say? She had me the first time she glared at me."

While Hunter laughed, Dex's cell phone rang. "Belmont."

"Dex, we got a couple of snowmobiles at the base of Bear Mountain. You think you can catch up and tell them they gotta call it for the day? At least until we can get some of the snow packed and adjusted? I'm afraid all that noise is gonna bring down the whole top."

"Yeah, I'll take care of it."

Fifteen minutes later, Dex and Bluebell had parked on the side of the road, just under the mountain, when a thunderous sound made his blood run cold.

He looked up and watched as a tidal wave of snow slid down the steep, rocky peak toward the bottom. Dex pulled out his binoculars, but he didn't need them to see the two machines racing away from the base, trying to beat the avalanche.

They disappeared into the snow and Dex sprang into action. As long as they had an air pocket, Dex had fifteen, twenty minutes to find them before they suffocated.

He called 911 and gave them the location as he pulled his snowmobile and sled out of his truck. Arming his own beacon, he secured Bluebell on the snowmobile, her vest and beacon activated as well.

"All right, girl, let's save some lives."

Allie had overslept a little, and used up all of Dex's hot water during her shower, but since he wasn't home, she figured it was fine. Besides, her cabin's power was still out, so he was kind of stuck with her.

Allie didn't really think he minded, especially given the things she had planned to do to him tonight after she got home from the hospital.

It was going to be her first day back and she figured she was about to have at least one heavy conversation with Hunter. She wasn't going to explain or make excuses, she was just going to be honest about her feelings for Dex. Considering she'd made no romantic moves toward Hunter for weeks, she didn't think he'd care, but still…she was a little stressed about the whole thing.

It took her longer than usual to get to the hospital, because she had to wait for Penny to show up to watch Kermit. She'd agreed to let Allie borrow her car for the day, but insisted they go shopping for a four-wheel drive for her this week.

Allie didn't have a problem with that at all.

She walked into her office and had barely shrugged out of her coat when Rebecca knocked on her door.

"Allie, prepare for incoming. We've got two snowmobilers who got buried in an avalanche at the base of the mountain."

"Thanks, Rebecca, glad to be back. Do they have it covered?"

"Yep, Dr. Gracin is standing by. Just wanted to let you know."

"Thanks. Did you have a good weekend?" Allie asked.

"I did, actually. Just normal family stuff. Hey, what happened to your hand?"

Allie had almost forgotten about the cut. "Oh, I sliced my thumb while cutting vegetables. No big deal."

"That's exactly why I don't cook. Well, I'll let you get back to it. I'm sure you've got lots to catch up on."

She did, and now it looked like she'd have to wait until Hunter wasn't knee deep in avalanche survivors to deal with one of those things.

The first kid had managed to break the surface of the snow by the time Dex reached him, although he was holding his left arm limply against his chest.

"You okay? What's your name?"

"I'm Graham, and I think I broke my arm. But my brother, Chris, I can't find him."

All right, time for Bluebell to earn her kibble. "Bluebell, find."

Bluebell jumped from the back of the snowmobile and sank into the snow. Dex used the snowshoes he'd strapped on to make a path less deep. In the distance, he could hear the sirens signaling help was coming.

Before too long, Bluebell gave an excited howl and started digging, diving headfirst into the snow.

An EMT on another snowmobile pulled up, and Dex waved, pointing to Graham. "Possible broken arm. The other rider is buried. If you get him out of here, we'll work on this."

Dex grabbed his snow shovel and started digging with Bluebell, yelling for Chris. After what felt like hours of work, he heard a voice hollering from below and Dex started using his hands. "Chris, start moving toward the sound of my voice. You're getting closer, man, just a little farther."

Finally, Chris broke through the snow, gasping, his arms flaying. "Get me the hell out of here!"

Taking the guy's arms, Dex pulled, dragging him out. Chris lay on the ground, breathing heavily. "Thank God, I thought I was going to die down there."

"Are you hurt?"

"Just my head. I think I flipped a couple of times."

"Okay, I'm going to strap you to the sled. Can you walk?"

Chris stood a little unsteadily, and Dex helped him to the sled before strapping him in. He waved toward a couple of EMTs headed back out.

"Let's go, Bluebell."

Dex took off, heading toward the road. He saw the EMTs

spin around and kick up snow. Other people were jumping up and down excitedly, and at first, Dex thought it was in celebration.

And then he felt it. The handlebars were shaking in his grip.

Because the ground was trembling.

Glancing briefly over his shoulder, he saw the second avalanche descending the mountain, gaining on their tail. His heart dropped out of his chest and hit the bottom of his stomach with a sickening thud.

"Shit. Hang on," he shouted, knowing Chris probably couldn't hear him. He pushed the speed, silently chanting, *Come on … come on.*

He was so close to safety, but he could feel the cold air at his back, the leaden snow reaching out for him. So he took a deep breath.

And waited for impact.

Chapter 24

WHEN HUNTER GOT the call, it felt like someone had taken a sledgehammer to his gut, making him want to hurl.

The second thought that raced through his head was Allie. Did she know?

At a full run, Hunter rushed into her office. She looked up from the paperwork littering her desk, much like she had the first time he'd seen her, only this time Hunter was there as a friend and nothing more.

"Allie…"

"Hey, aren't you waiting on an incoming trauma?"

"Yeah, but Allie, you should know—"

"Actually, if you got a minute, I should go first. I am so sorry, but I think it should come from me—"

His voice boomed in frustration. "Shut up and listen!"

Her jaw dropped in surprise, and while she was speechless, he finished. "There was a second avalanche while Dex was bringing in one of the patients."

The blood drained from Allie's face. "Oh, my God. Is he okay?"

Allie stood in the middle of the intake door, waiting for Dex, her whole body quaking with adrenaline.

Two ambulances carrying the injured teenagers pulled up, and as they unloaded them, wheeling them in side by side, Allie overheard one tell the other, "Man, that guy was a fucking badass. You should have seen him…."

The doors closed behind them, so she didn't catch the rest of the conversation, but she didn't need to. She knew enough about what happened to know exactly what she was going to do to said "badass."

Dex's truck pulled into the parking lot and he climbed out, all six-foot-plus feet of him perfectly healthy. Allie couldn't decide what she wanted to do to him more: kiss or kill him.

He caught sight of her and broke into a trot, a broad smile on his face.

"Allie, you are not going to believe what happ—"

Swinging her fist, she punched him as hard as she could in the arm. "Are you crazy? I heard all about it, you idiot! Why didn't you wait for help before charging off like the Lone Ranger?"

"Jesus, what is wrong with you?" he asked, rubbing his arm.

"You! You could have been killed."

"If I hadn't gone when I did, those guys would have been caught under a second avalanche and we might not have found them at all."

"And I'm glad that they're okay, but you"—she shoved him in his chest, frustration raging when he didn't move—"almost ended up buried. Do you know what the hell went through my head when Hunter told me that if you had been seconds slower you wouldn't have made it?"

"Allie, you know what I do for a living. It's not always going to be abandoned puppies and vehicle accidents."

Gripping his shirt now in her tight fists, she tried to shake him. "I know that, but you can't just jump into shit without thinking. Not now. Not after everything we've shared." Her voice broke, and she choked up, blinded by tears.

"Allie, sweetheart, I'm fine. I'm here."

His arms slipped around her, bringing her into his body, and she sagged against him. Her face buried in his shirtfront, she wrapped her arms around him and whispered, "I'm still mad at you."

"I know."

Dex knew that people were peeking out at them, but he didn't care. Allie's anger had surprised him, but nothing had prepared him for the hysterical woman clinging to him.

So many things went through his mind while he was waiting for the snow to overtake him, but at the forefront of his mind were thoughts of Allie. He was damn lucky to be here, to tell her how he felt about her.

In fact, he'd been so exhilarated to have made it, he hadn't even considered she might be upset.

"Okay, I need to say something for a minute. You're missing a few key facts about what went down. First of all, I watched the avalanche happen, so I knew where to find them. With an air pocket, someone buried in the snow can live fifteen, twenty minutes. So, time was ticking. Second, I had my beacon on, so even if I'd been buried, they would have eventually found me."

"That's"—sniffle—"not comforting."

"Woman, will you shut up and let me get this out?" Reaching between them, he tilted her chin up so he could smile down at her. "And lastly, no matter what, I was going to make it back, because I had something important to tell you."

She wiped at her tearstained face and looked back at him.

He kissed her lips, salty with her tears, and whispered, "That I love you."

Then she hit him square in his shoulder.

"Ouch! I tell you I love you and you hit me *again?*"

"You just have the worst timing. I'm ranting at you for scaring me and you think that's a good time to drop the L-bomb?"

Dex deflated slightly. "Hey, if you aren't there yet, it's okay."

"What? Of course I love you. Why do you think I'm so pissed? We just got started and I thought—"

Dex didn't let her finish, cutting off her anger with his mouth until she was leaning into him. When they finally broke apart, he pressed his forehead to hers and whispered, "I promise to be more careful in the future."

"You better, or next time, I will beat the shit out of you."

Dex chuckled before whispering in her ear, "Have I ever mentioned my dream girl looks like an angel and cusses like a sailor?"

"Hmmm…you may have mentioned that once. If she shows up, I promise to step aside."

"Awfully gracious of you. Angelic, perhaps."

Allie pulled away from him, shaking her head. "There you go with the cheesy lines again."

"I can stop if you want."

"Never, never stop."

Dex never intended to in the first place.

Will you marry me for $10,000,000?

Read on for an extract

IT WAS A Friday morning and Janey Ellis was running late. As usual. She prided herself on being so low maintenance that she could make it from bed to car in twelve minutes flat. The only problem was the getting-out-of-bed part. This morning she could barely drag herself to the shower, having spent the previous evening reading scripts until midnight. Flowerpot Studios had three new TV shows going to series this season, and she was expected to give notes on all of them today—*if* she made it to work in time for her first call.

Sebastian, her ex, used to call her a lane-change demon, and it was true: she would never let some boring gray Prius slow her down. Indeed, she was weaving west on Sunset so fast she would have missed the billboard if it hadn't usurped the one for *her* show. The bright-yellow ad was wrapped around one whole side of a fifteen-story building that until yesterday had promoted the cop drama *Loyal Blue. Loyal Blue* was the only successful TV show that Janey had developed to date—the one that looked like it was going to secure her job for the next few years. But it had been cancelled. The finale had aired.

It wasn't her fault. Shows got cancelled all the time, and shows ran for years with worse ratings than *Loyal Blue*. It was a crapshoot. Nonetheless, as Janey's boss had put it, "Money is money and failure is failure." The towering building that had once showcased her success now displayed two-foot-tall Crayola-green letters reading: WILL YOU MARRY ME FOR $10,000,000?

The message was so bold and unexpected that it distracted Janey from wallowing in the sad fate of *Loyal Blue*. This was quite a departure from the TV ads that rotated through this prime Hollywood ad real estate. Janey slowed to gawk. It had to be another reality dating show, right? She cursed herself for not having been the one to come up with it. But then she read the rest of the sign: CREATIVE, OPEN-MINDED BUSINESSMAN WITH LIMITED TIME AND DESIRE TO PLAY THE FIELD. THIS IS A SERIOUS PROPOSAL.

Janey chuckled to herself. It was just weird enough to be legit. Dude obviously had some cash—she'd seen the budget line for the lease on that billboard, and it wasn't cheap. Cars started to honk, and Janey realized the light in front of her was green. She hit the gas a bit harder than she meant to and hurtled through the intersection.

The billboard vanished from Janey's mind as she dashed across the studio lot and hurried into the Flowerpot offices, but not for long. Inside she was a bit surprised to see that everyone—executives and assistants alike—was gathered in her boss's office. Uh-oh. This couldn't be good. After dropping her bag in her office, Janey went to see what was going on.

The roomful of people was staring out the window. "You can see the back of the building, over to the right," an assistant was saying.

"Check out the gridlock," someone else said.

"What's going on?" Janey whispered to her assistant, Elody.

"It's an ad," Elody said. "A ten-million-dollar marriage proposal. It went up this morning and has already gone viral. Gawker says it's caused three fender benders so far."

"I saw it on my way in," Janey said, feeling briefly proud that, for once, she hadn't been the one in the fender bender. "It's got to be some kind of hoax."

"Or a publicity stunt," her colleague Marco said. "Some wannabe actor decided to go big or go home."

"I think it's romantic," Elody said.

A voice boomed over the rest of them. "It's a waste of time and money. This isn't a watercooler, people. It's my office. Out."

Inwardly Janey kicked herself at her mistake. Her boss, J. Ferris White, had been known to can people for taking lunch breaks. Not long lunch breaks. Any lunch break at all. And after the collapse of *Loyal Blue* she needed to get back on his good side. She ducked out of the office with everyone else, feeling twelve years old.

AT 11:00 A.M. on the dot Suze Lee allowed herself her first coffee break of the day. Redfield Partners, though a small venture capital group based in LA, prided itself on offering all the benefits of a big Silicon Valley tech company. Pool and Ping-Pong tables, a half court for basketball, a fully stocked kitchen. The free coffee was supposed to stimulate them to work longer and later, but Suze was pretty sure the excuse for frequent breaks had cut her colleagues' productivity in half. She therefore limited herself to two visits to the café every day, twenty minutes each. Just coffee, no snacking. Today something was different. The café was strangely quiet. The persistent ping-pong of the game that never seemed to cease was silent for once. Instead there was a cluster of people around one of the café tables, where Kevin sat with his laptop.

"I'm sure the guy is sixty years old and ugly as a dog, looking for arm candy," Emily said.

"No! People in the comments are saying that he's a tech billion-aire. Too busy to waste time dating," Kevin said. "I mean, for all we know, he's upstairs now, watching the Tweets roll in." The second floor of Redfield Partners was home to the executive suites, where the investing and operations teams of the firm had their offices (open concept, of course, but still a floor above everyone else). There they met with eager start-ups, counted their millions, and worked out daily in the on-site gym. It was easy to fit it all in when you knew you were set for life. Suze, Kevin, the ten other "entrepreneurs in residence," and the support staff were always encouraged to use the gym, but none of them ever did. Who wanted the hyperfit, life-balance-obsessed partners to see them panting on a treadmill at a slow jog? Instead they took ownership of the in-house café, some of them subsisting solely on its PowerBars and caffeinated beverages.

"Suze—you should totally apply," Meredith said.

Suze practically spat out her iced coffee. "What are you talking about? Why me?"

"Don't play dumb," Meredith said. "I have walked down the street with you. Every man we pass drools, and those are the ones who don't even know that you're brilliant."

"And you're nice. Mostly. A little uptight, but in a nice way," Kevin chimed in.

"Thanks?" said Suze.

"You're the hottest catch in LA," said Jeff.

There was an awkward silence. Jeff, the office IT guy, rarely spoke. When he did, it was always a little creepy.

"He's right," Meredith finally said. "A ten-million-dollar catch."

Suze rolled her eyes. "If that were true…wouldn't I have been caught by now?"

"For ten million dollars you might as well find out," said Kevin.

"CAROLINE! WHERE *ARE* YOU?"

Caroline Fried-Miller cringed. This was working out worse than she'd expected. She'd been living back at home for only two weeks, and already every word out of her mother's mouth got on her nerves. It was not a large house. And yet her mother had to bellow from downstairs as if they'd been separated at an oversold general-admission concert. At this rate Caroline would never last long enough to get back on her feet. Losing her apartment had been an unexpected blow. It was nobody's fault. It had been her roommate Angie's apartment first. Angie had landed the sweet, low-rent beach pad in Venice through a family friend. The lease was in her name. She paid all the bills, and Caroline reimbursed her. That was why it was totally cool when Angie's boyfriend, Bill, started living with them. It was fun, sort of like a super-crowded sitcom. But Caroline should have seen the writing on the wall. When Angie got engaged to Bill (Caroline was so happy for them! She really was!), of course they wanted Caroline out.

Finding a new place on her nonprofit salary wasn't going to be easy. She needed a second job, or something. Meanwhile, stuck at home with her mom and little sister, she was determined to keep the peace. The indomitable Isabelle Fried wasn't going to change. And Caroline was in no position to complain. She rolled out of bed.

"Be right there," she said politely, but at a proper volume that quite possibly would not reach all the way downstairs to her mother. Caroline was willing to be respectful, but that didn't mean she had to compromise her standards. She refused to turn into her mother.

"Hurry, look, you'll miss it!" her mother urged as Caroline came into the living room. "This is it, honey, your golden ticket!"

Isabelle was staring at the TV, where the local news was covering a story Caroline had glimpsed on her phone on the way downstairs. Something about a billboard with a marriage proposal.

"Mom, I am not Cinderella. Please don't fairy-godmother me."

"Don't be such a snob. It's fun. This man, whoever he is, is obviously smart, or he wouldn't be rich, and he's obviously determined, or he wouldn't be launching this impressive campaign. He knows what he wants and he's willing to pay for it. You should try out, honey. You've got nothing to lose!"

"Um…thank you for thinking of me, but I'm not for sale."

Isabelle shook her head. "Don't be obstinate. He's not buying *you*. He's buying opportunity."

Caroline laughed. "Okay, you win."

"So you'll do it. Great. The audition is tomorrow—"

"What? No!" Caroline shook her head. "You win that he's *buying opportunity*. You don't win entering me into the wife contest."

"Are you sure?" her mother asked. "You know, you haven't had a boyfriend since He Who Shall Not Be Mentioned. It's not like you have a good track record with finding your own boyfriends. Might as well put it in the hands of fate."

"Yeah. No."

Isabelle stared at her daughter. Then she got a glint in her eye. "Five hundred dollars," she said. "I'll give you five hundred dollars."

"Uh, Mom? I'm not an idiot. If I won't do it for ten million dollars, why would I do it for five hundred?"

"Because I'll give you the five hundred just for trying."

"Do I get five hundred dollars, too?" Caroline's little sister, Brooke, piped in from the doorway.

"Get ready for school, sweetie," Isabelle told her second daughter.

Caroline said, "How about you give me five hundred dollars to clean out the garage, which I've been doing in my spare time for two weeks now? Isn't that worth five hundred dollars?" She could really use the money. When she moved out, a landlord was going to ask for first month's rent and a month's deposit—cash she didn't have sitting around.

"Five hundred dollars to take a chance with Prince Charming. Deal or no deal?" her mother said.

"No deal." Caroline couldn't be bought by a man, and she certainly didn't want to be bought by her mother.

"I'll do it for two hundred!" Brooke said.

"Get your backpack, we're late," Isabelle told Brooke.

JAMES PATTERSON
BOOK**SHOTS**

OUT THIS MONTH

THE CHRISTMAS MYSTERY

Two priceless paintings disappear from a Park Avenue
murder scene – French detective Luc Moncrief is in
for a not-so-merry Christmas.

COME AND GET US

Miranda Cooper's life takes a terrifying turn when an SUV deliberately
runs her and her husband off a desolate Arizona road.

RADIANT: THE DIAMOND
TRILOGY, PART 2

Siobhan has moved to Detroit following her traumatic break-up
with Derick, but when Derick comes after her, Siobhan
must decide whether she can trust him again . . .

HOT WINTER NIGHTS

Allie Fairchild made a mistake when she moved to Montana,
but just when she's about to throw in the towel, life in
Bear Mountain takes a surprisingly sexy turn . . .

JAMES PATTERSON
BOOK**SHOTS**
COMING SOON

HIDDEN

Rejected by the Navy SEALs, Mitchum is content to be his small town's unofficial private eye, until his beloved 14-year-old cousin is abducted. Now he'll call on every lethal skill to track her down . . .

THE HOUSE HUSBAND

Detective Teaghan Beaumont is getting closer and closer to discovering the truth about Darien Marshall. But there's a twist that she – and you, dear reader – will never see coming.

EXQUISITE: THE DIAMOND TRILOGY, PART 3

Siobhan and Derick's relationship has been a rollercoaster ride that has pushed Derick too far. Will Siobhan be able to win back her soul mate?

KISSES AT MIDNIGHT

Three exciting romances – *The McCullagh Inn in Maine*, *Sacking the Quarterback* and *Seducing Shakespeare*.

SEDUCING SHAKESPEARE (ebook only)

William Shakespeare has fallen in love – with the beautiful Marietta DiSonna. But what Shakespeare doesn't know is that Marietta is acting a role. Unless Shakespeare can seduce her in return . . .

BOOKSHOTS

STORIES AT THE SPEED OF LIFE

www.bookshots.com